THE BEANO

THE BEANO

Rony Robinson

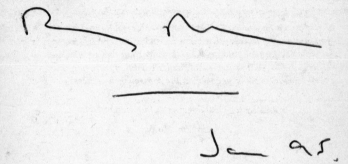

faber and faber

LONDON · BOSTON

First published in 1987 by
Faber and Faber Limited
3 Queen Square London WC1N 3AU
This paperback edition first published in 1988

Photoset by Parker Typesetting Service Leicester
Printed in Great Britain by
Cox & Wyman Ltd, Reading, Berkshire
All rights reserved

British Library Cataloguing in Publication Data

Robinson, Rony
The beano.
I. Title
823'.914(F)   PR6068.019/
ISBN 0-571-15232 5

For Lily

with thanks to Robert Cooper
and Christopher Honer

Contents

PART ONE

1

The Beano

The photograph – How the beano starts – The socialist and the landlady and the candle – The suffragettes who have never heard of Mrs Pankhurst – Mint imperials and wedding rings – Faint in the east behold the dawn appear! – Hopscotch and brandy at twenty to three.

The beano always ends with the photograph on the station.

But for obvious reasons this year's photograph is even more interesting than usual. And odd.

It is also fuzzy, so at first you think the brewery workers must all have shivered at exactly the same moment.

But then you see that the North Eastern Railways sign is fuzzy too. And so are the towers of pigeon baskets, and the dangling station clock, announcing thirteen minutes to seven.

Perhaps it's a very small sea fret? Odd.

It's more likely that the photographer was nervous.

But why should he have been? Just because there are three hundred clenched brewery workers a bottle-throw in front of him? The beanos always end like this, and the other photographs are not fuzzy.

And anyway this year he has two rows of railway workers between the camera and the mob.

Mind you, those railway workers in their smart uniforms look terrified, don't they? You would think they could pretend one last smile for the camera, this July evening, the moment before the brewery excursionists all go home for ever.

If they do all go home of course.

Peer as much as you like at the fuzzy photo, but you still cannot be sure who is going home.

The two lopsided drunks in the far corner look like the painters. But who is that young man in a woman's scarf holding hands with that bare-headed lass there? And who is that huge man pointing his fingers into his huge open mouth? Next to that woman who looks like the landlady of the Britlings pub next to the cemetery, with her hand on the arm of the man in the long buttoned mackintosh? Next to the sign saying 'Britlings' and the date?

He must be Mr Wagstaff of course, who organized it all. But he looks far too cheerful for him. What's he got to be cheerful about? And he's an unmarried Primitive Methodist. What's he doing with a pub landlady on his arm?

Odd.

And above all why does Mr Holles, the boss, look so desperate on his table in the very middle of this fuzzy beano photograph? As if he has glimpsed some sudden unthinkable future? Next to poor Mrs Holles – who is smiling! (Now what has she ever had to smile about?)

And where are the suffragettes from Washing?

And the entire Carpentry Shop?

And the Clarion socialist?

And can you be sure all the Chapel folk are present, when you count them?

Yes, it is an odd photograph, taken at thirteen minutes to seven, when there is nothing more to look forward to but the train home and work in the morning.

* * * * *

The beano starts seventeen hours earlier at quarter to two in the morning.

Listen to Mr Wagstaff's scratch silver band playing outside the brewery.

Only Mr Wagstaff and his megaphone are here watching them. And he is not at all cheerful now. He is so tired his eyes twitch in the cold morning.

His bandsmen wear uniforms from five different bands that might not be noticed in the gas-lamp light. But what they play will certainly be noticed. And even Mr Wagstaff can tell there is something wrong about that. There seem to be too many low sounds. And too many tunes.

It will be most unfair, Mr Wagstaff thinks, that when Mr Holles bothers to arrive, he will cause a fuss in front of the employees. For it was, after all, Mr Holles who sacked what was left of the brewery band after last year's beano. And he wouldn't pay them first. Just as it was, after all, Mr Holles himself who decided only yesterday that the beano couldn't possibly start without a band, and Waggy shouldn't be so mean with other people's money.

So there is a band to start the beano.

And Mr Wagstaff, in his mackintosh and megaphone, wishes it was over.

* * * * *

'That's the band, Mr Owen. And I've got your tie.'

Owen in the attic bedroom of 4 Windermere Street jerks awake in his chair at his table.

'I begged you not to get up for me, Mrs E.' He ruffles his hair. And the bed.

'I can't talk through doors,' she says through the door.

'It's not locked. I don't believe in locked doors. I don't believe in privacy.' But he is buttoning his trousers as he says so.

'That's your trouble, Mr Owen, you don't believe in nothing. Even God.'

'I believe lots of better things than Him. One, Labour is the hope of the world.' (He would believe that, wouldn't he? For Owen, of course, is the Clarion socialist who won't be on the fuzzy beano photograph tonight.)

'Are you respectable, Mr Owen?'

'Never.' He knots his red tie. 'I also believe in naturism and the liberation of the body from Victorian suffocations.' He flicks his foot on to the bed to buckle his sandal. 'Even our feet will be given their democracy.'

'I'm coming in regardless.' And she does. 'You've got your sandal on my bed.'

He removes it. The blowing candle-light waves their shadows together up the bare attic walls.

With her hair loose and her body still free of its Victorian suffocations so early this beano morning, she looks younger than he does. And he has never seen her bare feet before.

5

She says, 'You're staring at me.'

'I'm thinking how much I hate bands. All that heavy English certainty that nothing will ever change. But it will.'

She bends over the bed. She smells of warm oatcakes.

'You have not slept again. That's three nights this week, Mr Owen.'

'I'll pay extra for the candles, don't worry.'

'You're getting worse.'

'Things are getting worse.'

'And you're still staring.'

'Yes.' But he is unhooking his jacket from the nail now. 'There is so much work to do.'

'You're wearing your own mucky red tie I notice.'

'Yes.'

'You and your politics again.'

'Wearing the late Mr E.'s grey tie for the beano, like you want, would be politics too. Everything is. You either want to change things or you don't.'

She puts her hand on his arm. 'Why can't you enjoy yourself a bit more?'

'I want us all to. It's why I'm a socialist.'

She stares. The candle dances in her young eyes. She pinches him.

'I've told you I'm a pacifist too, so there's no point in hurting me.'

'There's no point in you going on this beano neither.'

'You mean only Tories like you are reckoned to enjoy themselves, Mrs E.?'

'I'm a non-political, Mr Owen, as you well know.'

'I can't see the difference.' He grins. 'It's still too dark.'

'I'll give you dark.' And the candle blows out. And Owen cracks his head on the sloping attic roof and sees bright morning stars.

* * * * *

And as the wind changes, you can hear Mr Wagstaff's band again, now marching up by the abattoir.

What shall we do? Stay here in the dark with Mrs E.? Or go off on the beano for a bit of a change? Oatcakes or revolution? What a question!

* * * * *

6

But we all have questions on beano morning.

That's why beanos are good for us. Go away and we can be someone else. Come back home and find all our questions answered.

Mind you, looking at that fuzzy photograph at thirteen minutes to seven tonight, you'd think there'd been some funny answers to some funny questions today.

* * * * *

Meanwhile, though, sixteen-odd hours before the photograph he will not be on tonight, Owen sways, slightly concussed, in his bedroom with his non-political landlady.

* * * * *

And there are some other brewery workers who look like missing the beano too.

Listen, for example, outside 347 Little Industry Road, where the three suffragettes who have never heard of Mrs Pankhurst snore and gurgle just above the gas lamp. As comfy as three bottles of Britlings Imperial XXX stout.

Bess, Edna and Ada, they are. Born the same year, within a mile of each other. And they have overlapped lives ever since, and stayed more or less friends too, even after that trouble three years ago. They're still friends enough to have signed on for the beano together, anyway, instead of washing bottles together in cold water and that chemical stuff that's made Bess's fingernails loose. And they are all snoring together now, in Bess's wedding bed, this very early morning, in case they oversleep.

Edna lies on her tummy in the middle, dreaming of Mr Holles the brewery boss. She shouldn't really be having such a dream of course, if they're going to be suffragettes all beano.

Which they are. Unless they miss the whole thing? For who's going to wake them up? The back-to-backs and courts and gennels and little industries in Little Industry Road all muffle the scratch band, now meandering up at the Rag and Tag Market where nobody needs waking anyway. The loudest sounds on Little Industry Road are from the suffragettes themselves, snoring and gurgling above the gas lamp with all the tea they drank last night.

Shall we go without them too? (They will not be on the

fuzzy photograph tonight either, will they?)

* * * * *

And what about Miss Tidmarsh from the office? Will she miss the beano, too?

Even though she is fully awake and dressed at five to two in the morning. In fact she's not been to bed at all, though early last night she did go up to her room, undress, and let her hair down. She then went down to kiss Pa on the forehead and say goodnight as usual. And then she went up to her room, waited a time and then started getting ready all over again.

But she still isn't going now.

Look at her. She's standing still at the front door of 17 Grove Avenue where she lives alone with Pa. She's listening to Mr Wagstaff's silver band, three miles away, but very clear in the black morning. She does not even notice how badly they play. Though she was going to be a concert pianist once.

She's talking to herself, between gulps of cold air.

'I'm going to go. I will not cry.'

The houses here at Grove Avenue, halfway up to the moors, have tiny front gardens held in with sharp spikes and hedges. You can smell heather and bilberries and perhaps even ozone, whenever the wind slices in from the east coast a hundred miles away, as the seagull flies.

But you don't make a fuss about it. You don't make a fuss about anything here in dusty Grove Avenue. You never drink beer here, even if you work in a brewery and you could get it free. And you are paid by the month even if you have to work. And your day begins half an hour later than the workpeople's. And very few people call you by your Christian name, though you go to church each Sunday morning. You are allowed to be ill, but quietly. You suffocate forgivingly here among the spluttering gas fires and the tonic medicines. You grow older faster here than your own parents.

And you talk to yourself on beano mornings, as Miss Tidmarsh is doing now.

'I am going to go. I will not cry.'

She shivers, pushes the front door softly shut and pulls the curtain across. She tiptoes down the hall past her silly beano hat on the hall table, waiting there with her satin specimen box, her church gloves, a quarter of mint imperials – and her mother's wedding ring.

'I am going to go. I will not cry.'

She tiptoes in to kiss Pa's forehead as he sleeps. But he is awake and staring.

She says, 'No, Pa, there is no rain. And I really must be going now.'

He says she is shaking. Why is she shaking? She knows she is not strong? She'll only get giddy again. And she isn't young any more, is she?

She tidies his medicines along the mantelpiece, making her fingers sticky again. She licks them. And she can smell her skirt scorching from the spluttering gas fire.

Look at yourself in the mirror, Miss Tidmarsh, in your respectable weekday office clothes. The white blouse with a crinkly blue cravat pinned at the collar. And the plain buckled belt, dark blue skirt with the four embroidered circles in the same colour so they will not need to be noticed. Your only extravagance this beano Friday is your Sunday shoes. Your hair is brushed up hard from your forehead as always and pinned tight, though there are as always a few escaping curls. And some grey now. The lips are too thin, the teeth too small and the skin too pale. But the brown eyes say, 'This woman has not given up. Not quite. Look!' Don't they? Look, they defy you. They say, 'Look at me. I am not plain. I am not dull. Unlock the pianos and tear down the curtains. Touch me.'

Her father says she is looking at herself in the mirror again, isn't she? She knows what happens when she looks at herself in the mirror. She knows what the doctor warned after last time. She'll be giddy.

She turns, her back to the fire and the mirror. 'I have not been giddy for a long time now, Pa. I will send you a picture postcard with all the news as soon as I arrive at our destination. You will not have to worry about me all day, and you can have a good rest for once.'

He says he does have to worry about her, doesn't he? She is his little girl, isn't she? What will he have to worry about if anything happens to her?

She says, 'I am thirty-eight. If anything were going to happen to me, Pa, it would have already happened.'

9

He says there is always next year, isn't there? For her anyway.

The Westminster chimes announce half-past two.

She says, 'Mr Holles is very keen that the monthly staff play their full part in today's outing. Especially, Mr Holles says, after Rhyl last year.'

He says she's a silly goose, isn't she? If it is only Mr Holles who is making her shake, then she must simply go back up to her room now and he will write to Mr Holles on Monday explaining it all, as he always has done whenever she has got into a pickle. Is Mr Holles why she is shaking? Or is there someone else?

Miss Tidmarsh blushes.

But she must go! She must not cry!

She kneels to move the saucer of water in front of his gas fire. She smells her hair burning. It does not matter. She must not cry. She must go. And most of all, now, she must not think about Mama's wedding ring, under the mint imperials. Taken off her dead finger the morning she left, without saying, and the piano stayed locked for ever.

But she must not think about that now. For Pa can tell what she is thinking. She can only have secrets that she never dare tell even herself.

He says she's having one of her giddy turns now, isn't she? Getting all hot and bothered like this? How can she possibly go anywhere today? Of course she is disappointed. He is disappointed for her. But other people live with disappointments, don't they? She must have a small glass of his tonic wine and go back to bed. If ever she went to bed in the first place, did she?

She crumples. 'I must go Pa! Please? I'm thirty-eight.' But she is crying great baby tears on to her crinkled blue cravat. And it's twenty-five to three.

He tells her to go up to her room at once.

'Yes Pa. I'm sorry Pa.'

* * * * *

Still, if you hurry back down to Windermere Street now, you'll just be able to see Owen in his red tie and sandals padding out of Number 4 into the gas-lamp light, in spite of his landlady.

10

And he's singing.

> 'England arise, the long long night is over,
> Faint in the east behold the dawn appear.'

Such an optimistic song, for there is not a skerrik of dawn this morning. And it's a long song, too, ideal for his long walk to the station as it is ideal for the Clarion rambles or for the ILP Sunday-school afternoons. Owen knows all twelve verses. Which is more than most English socialists ever do.

> 'From your wretched slums
> A voice of pity comes
> Arise O England for the day is here!'

At first he pads alone through the empty streets but as your eyes get used to the blackness you can see more excursionists keeping close to the houses and bending into the black wind.

> 'People of England all your valleys call you
> High in the rising sun the lark sings clear.
> Will you dream on, let shameful slumber thrall you?'

He reaches the end of Derbyshire Lane and pads up the gennel there, intending to cross Little London Road at Four Lanes End and then to walk across to the station via the footbridge.

> 'Labour is mocked, its just reward is stolen,
> On its bent back sits idleness encrowned.
> How long while ye sleep
> Your harvest shall it reap.'

And he comes out of the gennel and there is suddenly Mr Wagstaff's silver band, marching on the spot with torches and banners. And the brewery horses. And dozens of excursionists dancing and blocking London Road. And fighting. And five children are sucking oranges in front of the cornet player, so that his lips won't work.

Owen stops singing and turns towards the Bents and Howard Terrace. It will be about a mile longer but anything is better, on beano morning, than Mr Wagstaff's band. Northern bands, Owen decides, make the music of slaves. All that granite certainty in spite of all those wrong notes. All the half-religious beery patriotics, to keep the workers quiet as they bruise their lips on their cold cheap instruments, and give each other prizes, and never speak or create or change anything. All that noise to stop you thinking!

On the second day of the revolution the silver bands will be abolished! No, of course, when there is democracy, the bands will abolish themselves and the bandsmen will sing free.

And Owen suddenly thinks of Mrs E., and warm oatcakes.

> 'Forth then ye heroes, patriots and lovers!
> Comrades of danger, poverty and scorn,
> Mighty in faith of freedom your great Mother,
> Giants refreshed in joy's new rising morn!
> Come and swell – '

And in the dark of the new rising morn he walks into a beer crate on the causey edge of the Bents. He stubs his sandalled toe, rips the skin off his ankle and stumbles on to the pavement.

The beer crate belongs to Flossie the painters' ganger.

Flossie shouts, 'What are you kicking my beer for, Owensie? And talking to yourself?'

'Singing, Flossie.'

'Surprised you can hear yourself in all this chuffing row.' He sticks out his big warm hand for Owen to pull himself up.

'Ta, Flossie. On the second day of the revolution we'll abolish that chuffing row.'

'None of your politics.'

'Everything's politics.'

'Not on the beano.'

'The beano's politics.'

'That's politics.'

'Course.'

Flossie spits. 'No politics today.'

'That's politics too.'

'Right, so shut it. And give us a lift of my ale, instead of chuffing kicking it.'

They tug the crate to the next gas lamp. Flossie crumbles. When he can breathe again he pants, 'Old Waggy looked a bit peaky in his daft mackintosh, didn't he? Mester Holles hasn't turned up yet, see. You helping? Or what?'

They balance Owen's book and leaflets on the crate. Flossie gasps. He's thirty-seven, a year older than Owen, but he's already a gasping, windy man. He has his best jacket on, but it's his usual white silk scarf that's knotted tight under his chin and his usual cap that is too small and always falls off when there is work to do.

It falls off now.

He belches. 'I've been eating porridge all night to line me stomach see, Owensie. The wife always told me to get a good lining. Mind you she told me a lot of things. Bend! Up!'

He struggles the crate on to Owen's shoulder and follows, caressing the beer from behind. They shuffle into Devonshire Terrace.

'You never wed?' Flossie calls.

'No.'

'That with you being a socialist?'

'Part of it. But I've moved about too much.' And it is Owen who gasps now.

'My wife always reckoned I should have wed Albert.'

You can hear the gathering crowds at the station now. It is a low serious rumble, as hundreds of excursionists try not to get too excited in case it is still all a dream.

Owen clanks the crate down on to the causeway.

Flossie belches. 'What rubbish you got there then, Owensie?'

'Leaflets.' Owen gasps. 'And William Morris.'

'Taking them on holiday to chuck them in the sea?'

'To give to folk.'

'No folk like you at the seaside, Owensie.'

'We're everywhere.'

They carry the crate at knee level, for one gas lamp, till Flossie capsizes.

'No rush,' he puffs. 'Never thought I'd live to go on another beano, Owensie! Pity you're chuffing teetotal. Else I'd split a beer with you to celebrate. Hup!'

They surprise themselves, and the beer crate, and manage three gas lamps with it wobbling on Flossie's shoulder. Owen grabs it as it slides off and clanks on to the pavement. Flossie snorts for some time. Then says, 'Why didn't you stay at home with that widow woman of yours? Nobody'd have noticed today.'

'Give over, Floss.'

'She'll make you wed her. In due course, course. Socialist or not. And you don't believe in that. Like you don't believe in having fun.'

Owen says nothing. Oatcakes or revolution? It's that question Owen will be asking himself all beano.

* * * * *

If there is going to be a beano, that is.

For where is Mr Holles? This boss who hires and fires entire bands? And frightens Mr Wagstaff? And appears in suffragettes' dreams? And was so keen that the monthly staff play their full part today in view of what happened last year at Rhyl?

How can there be a beano without him?

Mr Wagstaff, still suffering with the band, tells excursionists who ask that he really hopes Mr Holles is not ill.

* * * * *

And Mr Holles is not ill, of course. He's never ill. Why should he be?

He is laughing now, playing hopscotch with his straw boater by the electric light from his conservatory in the garden up at The Lawns.

But he does seem to have forgotten the beano, as he hopscotches up the flagstones towards his wife while the plump new maid stares.

Mr Holles is a portly man, but he is almost dainty too, in his early fifties, dressed for this year's beano in an astonishing suit with wide checks. He is an energetic man who could easily dance all night at a Liberal function, with a woman almost young enough to be his daughter, and make her laugh so much she would agree to marry him, before she even asked her father.

(And that of course is what poor Mrs Holles did, five years ago.)

She is not laughing now, as she watches her husband hopscotch towards her up the paved path. But of course he is not doing it to make her laugh any more. She does not look young enough to be his daughter any more, either.

She is dressed in black for her beano, as if she is still in mourning for that father she exchanged for Mr Holles. And she is thinking of her father now. For, long ago, he took her to the same seaside the beano is going to. He showed her a skeleton there. And a bright white lighthouse. And a wooden pier on legs that went right out to sea. And he carried her back along it. Singing? Because something had happened? If she could ask her father he'd remember. But of course she can never ask him anything again now.

She calls, 'Mr Holles I really think I must have a word with you in private.'

He jumps. 'I am aware Mrs Holles that you do not wish in your present bilious state to have to gallop down to the railway station.'

'I merely –'

'Merely don't, Mrs Merely Holles.' He tiddlywinks his boater with his brown shoe. He skims it at the Girl, who curtsies and bends to pick it up. He looks at her, though he speaks to his wife. 'I am playing hopscotch now while I wait for *The Times* newspaper to arrive with a boy on a bicycle from the railway station as specially arranged, for this special beano morning. *The Times* newspaper is my atlas of the empire of commerce, and the bible of my trade. I am aware, Mrs Holles, that commerce and trade make you bilious.' The Girl hands him his boater. He puts it on and taps it. 'The thought of a long train journey to the east coast with you, but without a newspaper, makes me a little bilious too.'

He strides to the edge of his garden, and looks down at his town. He can just make out the shape of his brewery and his river. He listens for his brass band, rasping everybody awake whether they are going on his beano or not.

But the wind is blowing down from the moors now, cold and northern, and he hears nothing.

He fumbles in his secret inside pocket of his astonishing beano suit. He shouts, 'I will merely say this, Mrs Holles. If *The Times* does not arrive for the beano, then the beano is merely cancelled.'

He uncaps his silver flask and drinks to the coming morning.

And the morning should be coming by now, at just after twenty to three. But the sky is still dead.

2

Time to Go

The Irish Clock – Miss Tidmarsh arrives with her mint imperials – A shambles threatens – Percy from Cooperage and Lizzie from Hop Stores, and the Japanese Lake, the cake and the hat box – The stowaways – A song for the thirsty of Macedonia – The painters' occupation – The Arrival – Lizzie introduces Percy while denying she is a paradigm of pulchritude – They're off.

'That the time?'

'Must be.'

The great black-and-white clock that dangles over the Midland Station forecourt says twenty minutes to three.

But it isn't.

The clock is three minutes slow. And has been since it fell on the Irishman who was putting it up in 1881. Many trains have been missed because of him, though real travellers know that the Irish Clock cannot be trusted. But the Irish can't, can they? They'll be having their civil war any day now, judging from what the papers say.

Still, there are more things to worry about than the Irish, this beano morning.

'Is that you, our kid?'

'Depends who you are.'

There are far too many of us trying to push and squeeze under the Irish Clock where we all said we'd meet each other. And even when we can squeeze in, we're unrecognizable, in our Sunday hats and veils and behaviour. And new haircuts and closest shaves, too, for the beano is the best day of the year to get shorn, ready for the ozone and sunshine.

'What kind of day you reckon we're going to get?'

'Can't tell while we get some daylight can you?'

You can't. So you have to bring every kind of clothes for every kind of weather, all worn in layers under borrowed overcoats so they don't count as luggage.

'Anyone seen my missis?'

'I've lost mine and all. What's yours look like?'

'Nothing on earth this morning.'

And there are too many shadows from the hanging gas mantles, and we all look like skulls.

And it's far too early anyway. Once we get going and the sun rises we'll be able to see who's come, and what kind of day we are going to have.

But listen to that beer crate on that man's head. It's cooing, at quarter to three this sober morning. Feel under the hanky that covers it – and you'll stroke a pigeon.

Stick a hand carefully into all the other gutted Britlings beer crates, and you'll finger pork pies and caraway seed cakes and pepper cakes and cold Yorkshire pudding and boiled eggs and pig-bag and parkin and pikelets and black pudding and bread-and-dripping and cold tea and pickled everythings, whole beetroots and dead rabbits.

And oranges! You can smell them everywhere.

And mothballs. And lavender.

'All right?'

'You?'

Lift your hat in the crush, and say good morning to everyone.

Be glad you've got your hat too. Because everyone else has. And if you don't wear a hat this dark morning, who can take their hat off to you? So they'll all be better than you, and you don't want that on beano day.

'Ding-ding, we're off.'

The stern Midland bell is ringing. And the stern Third Class excursionists' gate is opening. And Third Class excursionists can now present their tickets and themselves in an orderly way, and prepare to proceed to Platform 4, to bring credit to themselves and Britlings by both their behaviour and their attitudes, as described in the Illustrative Programme most of us have left at home anyway.

17

Touch your hat at the ticket collector.

'Morning, love, we'll bring you back a mermaid.'

'What use is mermaids, they're all fish where it matters.'

Go up the platform to get a seat. Not too near the front, for when the train crashes. Or the back, for when it's hit. And make sure you're facing the sea.

* * * * *

Only seventeen minutes to go now.

But look! Isn't that Miss Tidmarsh from the office, with her silly hat, guidebooks and mint imperials, pecking her way through the crowds, and pretending she doesn't exist?

So, Miss Tidmarsh is going on the beano after all! Does Pa know?

And does he know she's not going on her own either? For look at her now, as she veers to her right, and pecks her way briskly to the 'Parcels' notice and says, 'Mr Shephard, I'm here.'

And Mr Shephard from the office hears her still small voice through all the early morning beano. He touches his hat with his gloved hand, then his spectacles, and his book. But he does not touch Miss Tidmarsh as he murmurs, 'Ah. Miss Tidmarsh. Here we are.'

They are silent and still, after all the effort. They do not look at each other, for they are afraid to be seen. But there is no pair in England rejoicing more at being together this early morning, though their faces are taut with the pain of it all.

For Miss Tidmarsh loves Mr Shephard. And Mr Shephard loves Miss Tidmarsh.

Nobody has ever said so. They haven't even said so to themselves.

Miss Tidmarsh murmurs, 'I really did not think I was going to be able to extricate myself at the last moment, Mr Shephard. Pa was very difficult.'

Mr Shephard murmurs, 'Mummy was not at her most helpful this morning.'

'I am so sorry I am late.'

'It matters not a jot, Miss Tidmarsh. Mr Holles has not arrived yet. And I have spent the last few minutes most profitably consulting the Illustrative Programme about the times of the tides on the east coast. There appears to be a low tide just after eleven.'

18

He closes his Illustrative Programme, folds his spectacles into their case, and scoops the other three guidebooks he has been clutching between his knees.

'Would it be too early, do you think, for a mint imperial?'

'By no means. I am sure nobody is interested in us eating a mint imperial.' But he looks round to be sure. He takes off his glove to pluck a mint. And wonders if he dare ask Miss Tidmarsh, now, what he must ask her some time today? Get it out of the way now? Know exactly where they both stand?

But he drops his glove. 'Oh dear.'

* * * * *

Eleven minutes to go.

And look, here's Mr Wagstaff arriving in his long mackintosh with the band and the brewery horses and the laughing excursionists sucking oranges.

'What sign of Mr Holles?' he asks the jolly party from Electric Light, eating black pudding by the horse trough.

'Not lost him have you, Mr Wagstaff?' And they laugh in a jolly way.

Mr Wagstaff never laughs, and certainly not on beano morning. He orders the band and the brewery horses to hide opposite the station in Little Jericho. And to wait there in silence until Mr Holles arrives in his motor car. 'You are then to march briskly over, playing whichever tune you play best. If any.'

The band and the horses hide. Mr Wagstaff shakes hands with the Station Master in striped trousers and bowler.

'No sign of Mr Holles, Station Master?'

'Indeed not, Mr Wagstaff. And he must be due.'

The Station Master's daughter curtsies and offers a bouquet of roses to Mr Wagstaff, who takes them. The Station Master smacks her with the crown of his bowler. 'Wrong destination.' He gives the bouquet back to the girl, and leads Mr Wagstaff to the porter's trolley by the First Class entrance to the platforms. There is a carpet on the trolley and Mr Wagstaff steps on to it. Six senior porters wait at the side in a line with a carafe of water, a wicker hamper, a carpet and two glasses.

Only nine minutes to go now.

The Station Master checks his watch. 'He's running late.'

Mr Wagstaff climbs on to the porter's trolley. He grips his megaphone and shouts. 'I must remind excursionists that Third Class passengers are allowed neither luggage nor livestock, and should now be proceeding in an orderly way, bringing credit to themselves and Britlings, as clearly laid out in the Illustrative Programme.'

And Flossie was right. Mr Wagstaff does look peaky in his raincoat. But wouldn't you? There are so many ways a beano can become a shambles. Last year the train did not come . . .

'You do have a train for us this year, Station Master?'

'He's a-drinking and a-steaming on the Up platform, Mr Wagstaff, and he can't wait for his holidays.'

'But no Mr Holles?'

'Trouble on the track? Unavoidable delay, Mr Wagstaff?' The Station Master pokes his daughter-with-the-flowers with the brim of his bowler. 'They're not for your refreshment neither.'

Mr Wagstaff raises his famous megaphone. 'I must remind excursionists that once you are aboard you are not to arrange yourselves horizontally on either seats or luggage r—'

For Mr Wagstaff has faltered on a thought so terrible he hardly dares to think it. But just suppose Mr Holles has got the wrong day?

'Would you care to come to my office for a smallish brandy, Mr Wagstaff?'

'I am a teetotaller, Station Master.'

'You're looking peaky, sir. Think of it as medicine.'

'I have had an intimation, Station Master, that this year's beano will be the last.'

The Station Master looks at his watch, and the Irish Clock. Mr Wagstaff feels less cheerful than ever. The daughter is now eating Mrs Holles's roses again. The Station Master notices her, but he does not bother to smack her any more.

* * * * *

Ten minutes to three by the Irish Clock, and twenty-two-year-old Lizzie from Hop Stores bangs her hat box through all the excitement up to twenty-three-year-old Percy from Cooperage.

And pokes him in the bum with it. 'Morning, you.'

'Bunty!' Percy calls, and turns so fast his stiff collar grazes his red neck. 'Oh, it's only you, Lizzie.'

And it *is* only Lizzie, smelling of too much lavender. Sweating now with all the rush and the weight of her hat box. And herself. In a pink headscarf. Whereas Percy is very ironed and grown up in his proper man's suit with his folded green cloth over his arm.

'Let's get on the platform, Percy, and get a place to sit.'

'You're not sitting with us, Lizzie.'

'Me mam's done us a fruit cake and a dozen macaroons. We can have them for breakfast.'

Percy turns away, scraping his neck again. He stares round on tiptoe to see where Bunty is.

But she isn't.

'Bunty and me don't want you tagging after us all day neither, Lizzie,' he says. 'We're doing some talking today.'

'That why you brought your mam's tablecloth?'

Percy turns and the collar tears his neck. 'I'm going to treat her to a canoe on the Japanese Lake if you must know. Ask her something somewhere she can't laugh and run off. And what's up with you now?'

For Lizzie is snatching at his grown-up suit. 'I've dropped me ticket, Percy! You'll have to bend!' She pushes him down among the crowd. Just in time to miss seeing the party of First Class travellers sweeping towards the First Class entrance. There are five of them – a cocky young man in a blazer, three elderly aunts with their handkerchiefs out, and a young woman in a veil.

Lizzie nods at the young woman, though she cannot see her face.

She keeps Percy pressed down in the crowd until the First Class party are safely through the barriers.

* * * * *

Only six minutes to go.

But such excitement here on Platform 4! It is hard to stay orderly in all the wonderful smells – hot oils, grease, disinfectant and brown parcels.

The shining scarlet coaches of the beano special are almost full now. And the hissing scarlet locomotive out beyond the roof is squirting all the children, who will grow up to be train drivers now, as well as soldiers and nurses. Or so they are telling their dads.

As three children without dads meet up by the Third Class Gentlemen's near the guard's van.

These are the stowaways, Tommy, Spud and Monkey. Aged twelve or thirteen. All pale with big tired eyes.

'We're not taking Monkey with us!' Spud says.

'Wait on, Spud.'

Monkey sits on the cold platform with one hand clenched on his bare knees and the other in his ragged trouser pocket. Spud has more clothes, though they are all two or three years too big for him. Tommy is all in squeaking corduroys and the most grown up of the three.

Tommy punches Monkey's shoulder. 'How do you get on the platform?'

'I come in through the ticket gate with a missis I asked. She said I was sweet, Tommy.'

'Me and Spud have been crawling down that track from the cutting since yesterday teatime.'

Spud spits on Monkey's boot. 'It's easy for him cos folk feel sorry for him cos he looks mental, Tommy.'

They skulk over to a massive tin poster for Pears soap that does not irritate children's delicate skin nor make their little eyes smart.

'How much brass you got, Monkey?'

'Nowt, Tommy.'

Spud spits at the Pears poster. 'I'll kill him if he comes with us.'

Monkey says, 'The missis give me a free go at that chocolate, Tommy.' He opens his fist to show six flat squares of gold and purple Nestlés chocolate.

'If you come,' Tommy says, 'no being daft, less Mester Waggy sees me. If he does you have one of your fits while I've run off.'

'Yeah, Tommy!'

'Mental,' Spud says, grabbing three chocolates.

'And shhh. I can hear a hymn.'

* * * * *

And he can, two minutes before we're off.

For in the smoky front carriage a party of Britlings Chapel folk sit obediently side by side and begin to sing of faraway countries:

'There's a cry from Macedonia, come and help us.
The light of the gospel bring, Oh come!
Let us hear the joyful tidings of salvation,
We thirst at the living spring.'

* * * * *

'Thirst? They don't know what thirst is, that lot,' Flossie yells.
He is leaning out of the carriage, keeping out the other
trades.

There are only four painters at Britlings now – so each has a
corner, on the beano. Flossie and Albert are at the window.
Old Spaldy is smearing ointment from a tube into the corner
of his eye. And Owen, in red tie, opposite, is thinking that
Flossie was right when he said it would be marriage, sooner
or later with Mrs E. And, with marriage, Owen would
become another of those who still talk about changing things
but really just try to be happy in private ... Oatcakes or
revolution though – what a choice!

Albert cries, 'Time we was off.'

'Time we had a drink,' Flossie belches. 'Whoops. I'm still
not right after all that porridge.'

And a respectable time-served bricklayer in a bowler veers
off and goes up the train for a more respectable carriage.

* * * * *

And there are no minutes to go now.

And Mr and Mrs Holles and the Girl gallop into the empty
station forecourt in the Stanhope gig, full of leather luggage.
Mr Holles is standing, poking the foaming horse with a
long-handled whip.

'Come on, earn your hay and corn you!'

The beano is on!

Mr Wagstaff picks up the megaphone. 'Your attention
please, Britlings employees. Please show your appreciation
now for – '

The band tumbles over from Little Jericho, waving their
instruments and cheering. They might get paid after all. The
Station Master steps forward two paces, followed by the six
senior porters, as choreographed by Mr Wagstaff, and rehearsed last Monday.

But Mr Holles only slashes at his horse, swerves the gig
through ninety degrees and gallops at the open Parcels gate.

Mr Wagstaff calls, 'Perhaps the initial welcoming ceremony could proceed from here, Mr Holles, as announced in the progr—'

But Mr Holles has gone. And, instead, there are the three chunky suffragettes from Washing sweating up, arm-in-arm. So they did wake up! (So why aren't they on the photo at the end?)

Edna yells, 'Morning, Waggy!'

Mr Wagstaff sweeps his megaphone round to them. 'Hurry along, you Britlings people. There really is no acceptable excuse. The excursion is preparing to depart.'

'Thanks for holding it up for us then, Waggy,' Edna yells from the barrier. And then, 'Ow Ada, will you give over pulling my hair.'

'You give up talking to men then.'

Mr Wagstaff shouts. 'All employees however humble are reminded that today they are ambassadors not only for themselves but also for Britlings Limited, and that at all time – '

But there is no time.

The Station Master shakes his head. 'I got you your train, Mr Wagstaff. I got you your departure hamper. And your floral tribute. What's left of it. Your Mr Holles is not on my roster.'

'Where's he gone?'

* * * * *

He's gone a-trotting down Platform 4 with poor Mrs Holles and the Girl and all the luggage. Look at him standing up waving *The Times*, and his straw hat, and steering the gig one-handed up to each cheering window to display this year's amazing beano suit, and poor Mrs Holles, and the plump maid without a coat.

And look now as he pokes his horse to a tittup down the platform, all the way to the scarlet engine where the animal rears up. Poor Mrs Holles and the Girl shoot forward on to the floor of the gig. Mr Holles snorts, and whips the steaming locomotive and its fireman leaning out of his cab in his little blue jacket.

Whatever will Mr Holles do next? What a card!

And how strong he is. Look at him drag the horse around, scraping its terrified hooves along the platform till they spark, then slithering and galloping it back towards Mr Wagstaff's band, now blocking the path by First Class Waiting.

Watch Mr Holles lean from the gig to snatch the chained silver whistle from a guard as the band begins the patriotic medley.

'Whoah!' Watch Mr Holles drive into them. He heaves the reins and once again poor Mrs Holles and the maid bounce forward and back. The horse slobbers and shakes sweat over the musicians. They play on, perhaps remembering their fellow musicians on the *Titanic* a couple of years ago who went on blowing and scraping because it was only a nightmare wasn't it and they knew they'd get paid if they managed to still be playing when they woke up . . .

'Mr Holles sir, if you would care to use this megaphone made last year by our own blacksmiths for the Rhyl outing?'

'We all remember the Rhyl outing last year, Waggy. Those of us who survived. Do you know how to stop that noise? We don't want rain before we even start.'

The players lower their instruments and drip on to the platform.

'Britlings!' Mr Holles now shouts. Excursionists in each carriage fight for the window. 'I had planned a few words of gratitude. But poor Mrs Holles here is bilious and has little gratitude for the Almighty's mercy in sparing us for another – Britlings Brewery Beano!' (Great cheers! It's beginning to feel like a beano now!)

Mr Wagstaff glances down at his pocket-watch.

'You're in a hurry to get us to the seaside again, Waggy?' Mr Holles cries. 'So you can drown us again and get the full value on the insurance?'

'I was wondering, Mr Holles, if – '

'Don't wonder. Daddy is speaking. Now, fellow members of the great Britlings family,' (cheers) 'no speech but three warnings. One there is to be absolutely no drinking of beer' ('aaaahhh') 'unless it's Britlings beer!' (great cheers). 'Two, I shall be making my address to the Almighty on our arrival at the seaside. I expect He'll be there. He doesn't have a Waggy to make a shambles of things.' (Laughter) 'I've given our Waggy the clearest orders about unloading when we arrive, remembering what the raggety business led to at Rhyl. No doubt he's told you there's to be no mafficking about.' (Murmurs) 'So no doubt it'll be even worse than last year!' (Cheers) 'And three we can't go anyway.' ('Aaaahhh!') 'I have not yet received the token of their regard for me from the railway company. I hope it is that hamper of rich food and drink for me to guzzle in the First Class all the way to the seaside? And that little girl there, with a chewed bouquet of flowers, which will only bring the first Mrs Holles here up in one of her rashes.' (Laughter)

What a card!

The Station Master knocks his daughter with his bowler. He signals the porter to wheel the wicker basket to the engaged First Class Lavatory carriage in the very middle of the train.

Mr Holles hands the Girl down then leaps off himself, almost seesawing poor Mrs Holles on to the platform.

'Come on, missis, we're off.'

* * * * *

And we are.

Almost.

Flossie the painter tugs the window shut with the leather strap, and gasps back on to his seat as his cap falls off. 'Have to admit it, Owensie,' he tells the Painters' Only carriage, 'our Mr Holles might be the boss but he's a right card, isn't he? Remember all that business in Rhyl with them basket chairs? And Lake Windermere when he dressed up as that nun? Mr Holles, eh!'

Mr Holles, eh!

* * * * *

And just look at him now, being a guard on the running board of his First Class Lavatory carriage with poor Mrs Holles and the Girl trapped safely inside behind him.

'You're late there.' He's seen Percy rushing along with his rug, poking into every Third Class, looking for Bunty. 'Dock him half a day, Waggy.' And then, 'And that's Lizzie, waddling up behind you! Lizzie, you paradigm of pulchritude!'

'It's not luggage, Mr Holles,' Lizzie gasps. 'It's only a hat box.'

'I hope you are all impressed I know Lizzie's name.' Mr Holles calls. 'Memory's a wonderful faculty when correctly used. Been keeping us waiting making yourself glamorous, eh Lizzie?'

'Me, Mr Holles?'

'You've no doubt done your – Britlings Best, eh?' (Cheers)

'Yes, sir.'

'This is the best you can do for a young man? His collar's a bit tight. His neck'll be bleeding by York. To say nothing of the damage he'll do himself when he's off tromboning in the courting hour – eh?'

'He's Percy, sir, from Cooperage. Just finished serving his time.'

'He'll be getting man's wages next then, thinking of getting wed?'

'He is sir, aren't you, Percy?'

Mr Holles thwacks Percy's bare head with *The Times*. 'There's lads coming out of that board school every year can do your work for quarter the rate.'

Percy says, 'Thank you, sir. I hope you have a pleasant and well-deserved holiday, Mr Holles.'

'Like ballocks you do.' Mr Holles holds his rolled paper behind his back. 'Besides, the weather is going to be appalling, listen! *The Times* says, and this is word for word mind you, by rote memory, "All parts of the United Kingdom except the western channels and bay, westerly and north westerly winds, fresh and strong at times locally. Gusty, changeable, showers. Continuing cool." Give you that for nowt, Percy from Cooperage.'

'Thank you, sir.'

'Wonderful thing memory, correctly used. Oh, and Lizzie?'

'Sir?'

'I'll give you something too. Fact from *The Times*. There are exactly one million two hundred thousand more women of marriageable age in Britain than there are young men for them.'

'Are there, sir?' Lizzie asks, disturbed.

'It's why I'm taking two women to the seaside. I'm going to share myself round a bit like the Liberals say you have to. If you want your share, get in.' He slams his door and leans out. 'This a beano, Waggy, or a shambles?'

'A shambles, sir, shouldn't we be – '

'We are!' Mr Holles blows the whistle. 'You've missed it, Waggy!'

Mr Wagstaff hurries down the platform as the band begins 'God Save The King' without being asked.

* * * * *

They play, thinks Owen, red-tied and sandalled in the Painters Only Third Class, as if even they are republicans and atheists under their servile uniforms – just like he is.

There is hope everywhere, if you listen for it.

* * * * *

'Here!'

Lizzie pushes Percy with her hat box into the unpopular Third Class next-but-one to the front. She tugs the door shut behind them. In the far corner there's a thin mother breast-feeding a baby with teeth. An ancient blacksmith opposite her blows at his black pipe stem and dribbles. 'Blocked up, isn't it a bugger.'

Percy pushes past Lizzie, back to the window. 'Will you stop mithering me, Lizzie?' He leans out.

'Listen, Percy. Bunty isn't coming. And – '

'She'll be waiting for me under that Irish Clock. And – ' But there are no more ands.

For the train jolts backwards and the coaches clash. Cheers! The train jerks forwards and shudders and judders. Another cheer, and some screams.

'We're off, Percy!'

And at last we are.

Percy stays leaning out.

The mother pokes Lizzie, and mouths over the train noise, 'Nice bum he's got your young man.'

'I know,' Lizzie says.

Four bridges later Percy turns round all smoky.

'What you crying for, Perce?'

'Got a smut in me eye.'

'Come and sit here. I've brought a clean hanky, special.'

He shakes his head and slings his mother's tablecloth into the net luggage rack. And he rubs both eyes with his fists.

* * * * *

It is nineteen minutes past three.

So the beano is only nineteen minutes late in setting off this year.

The jolly excursionists from Electric Light and their jolly

wives, in a Third Class near the back, begin the medley of train songs they will sing all the way to York without running out of steam.

> 'She arrived at Euston by the midnight train,
> But when she got to the wicket there
> Someone wanted to punch her ticket.
> The porters came round by the score
> And she told them all she never had
> Her ticket punched before.'

* * * * *

You can see those jolly Electric Light people and their jolly wives, still not run out of steam, on the fuzzy photograph right at the end of the beano. Fancy going all that way just to come back home the same as you went!

Still, it's better than not coming back home at all. And some of us are going to be missing by six forty-seven . . .

Anyway, no point in being morbid, yet. We're off, aren't we?

PART TWO

3

They're Off!

A Winter Warmer to start the day – Pickpockets, pies, wasps
and skirts – Secrets of the Ladies Only – The song that is
only sung once a year – Why the painters should be at home –
Into the tunnel – The blacksmith asks for help – Mr Holles
makes a suggestion about the maid's legs – The Crooked Spire
and the Lagoons of Liquorice – What to look forward to at York.

'You on, Albie?'

'Aye, why not?'

It's twenty to four, time to start drinking in the rocking painters' carriage.

'We'll start with a Winter Warmer,' Flossie says and plucks a bottle from the crate. He strokes it with his white scarf.

Albert grunts, 'You reckon that lot'll last while the seaside?'

Flossie stabs his knife into the first of the twenty-four corked bottles and his cap falls off.

'It's only you and me boozing it. Spaldy there daren't 'cos of his eyes. With Owensie it's his daft politics, of course. Eh Owensie? Shut it – no politics.' He sharpens his knife on the window strap. 'I didn't reckon old Owensie would turn up today, mind you, what with the beano being a trick by the bosses.' Flossie strokes the blade with his thumb. 'And what with his widow woman too, eh?'

Albert chuckles. 'Your cap, me old.'

'Ta.' And then, 'Owensie's neighbours tell me he's on that nest all night. Up in his attic there? His candle burning away all night, eh?' Flossie stabs and unplugs the cork. 'Cheers.'

'That's it.'

They drink the marmalade ale and do not speak for fifteen miles.

Then Flossie opens the door, and chucks the bottle at a coal train in the early morning. 'Another?'

'Aye.'

A bottle of Coronation Porter later, Flossie says, 'They're a right pair, these two. One comes beanoing to read books and one to paint chuffing pictures.'

'Aye, well.'

'You'd think we see enough paint all year without bringing it with us to the seaside.'

'You could say that about beer, Floss.'

Flossie opens the door and chucks the empty Coronation Porter bottle at a bridge. 'Smell that morning! Countryside, that. Fancy another, Albie?'

He does. They drink an Export Extra.

Then Flossie says, 'So this widow woman of yours has not come round to your ideas on free love yet then, Owensie?'

Owen shakes his head, reading.

'Thought not. She were in my Sunday school,' Flossie says. 'So she still charges you rent, eh? And course you socialists don't like rent, eh?'

Owen shakes his head.

Albert says, 'He's reading, Floss.'

And Flossie snarls, 'We'd all like to read.'

* * * * *

Mr Holles likes reading, and is doing so in the silent First Class Lavatory carriage, all walnut and lamps and footrests.

It's five past four now on this July morning, and ten minutes to sunrise according to *The Times*.

If the train keeps going straight the sun will be rising on Mr Holles's right, for he is, of course, facing the engine, and the sea. And his women.

We should be able to watch the sun, there beyond that coal mine in the middle of that long pale field fenced in by the last of the elderflowers, sooty now from the trains, and a few quiet poppies and all the wispy rosebay willowherbs.

Mr Holles is not watching. He is concentrating.

The Girl sits opposite him, black, white and plump,

34

looking at her plump fingers in her warm lap.

Poor Mrs Holles sits next to her, so she also has her back to the engine, bilious or not. She sits upright with her eyes closed and remembers the last holiday her family had together. Though they did not know it was the last then, of course. You never know what's coming next. And you can do nothing about it. They had rented that house in Robin Hood's Bay that year, hadn't they? But one day her father took her, just the two of them, on an adventure. They had sandwiches for breakfast! And they sat in the little train that smelt of paraffin and ran right along the edge of the sea. And there was a big white lighthouse that hurt her eyes when they got there. And it rained. And she wore his waistcoat. And there was a skeleton! And that long pier he ran carrying her down. It smelt of – tar and wood, didn't it? And she said the pier was a bridge!

Mr Holles shouts, 'How's the biliousness, Mrs Holles?'

Poor Mrs Holles's eyes flutter.

'She was asleep.' Mr Holles passes *The Times* to the Girl and bites into a spurting pork pie. 'Page five now, next to some girl who claims she was pickpocketed on a tram. You'll find news there of "10,451 dead queen wasps" which I have just memorized perfectly. "Great slaughter of wasps. At the Whitley Surrey Flower Show. 10,451 dead queen wasps were pinned on cardboard and exhibited." Yes? "Special prizes were given for their capture by Mr Joseph King. The chief wasp slayer was F. Snodgrove. No, Snelgrove. Who had 3,100 wasps to his credit." Yes?'

'Yes, sir.'

'Why do you keep tugging at your skirt?'

'Sir?'

'I've got Mrs Holles's legs to look at when I need to look at legs. Now turn to page seven because you will find, thanks to my study of Pelmanism, I also have a perfect mnemotechnic memory of the operation on Queen Augusta Victoria performed yesterday by Sir Bernard Dawson.'

And he has!

* * * * *

The three chunky suffragettes from Washing (who've never really heard of Mrs Pankhurst, let alone Queen Augusta

Victoria) are the only passengers in the Ladies Only carriage, five back.

'Some cold tea to go with that bacon, Ada?'

'Love some, Bess.' She chews and adds, 'If we'd not got so snudged up in that bed of yours we might have had time for some proper breakfast at your house.'

'Can you unscrew the bottle, love, me fingers are hurting again.'

Edna says, 'No tea for me, thank you.'

'You love your tea, you?'

Edna shakes her head and is tragic. 'I do, Ada, but I don't want to go.'

'Well, we are going. Else them trees are going backwards.'

'I mean – go . . . my trouble, Ada?'

'Our trouble, more like.'

Edna tuts. 'If I hadn't had to go when we was in Bess's bed we'd have missed the beano. It's my water trouble you've got to thank for being here.'

Three miles later, Ada says to Edna, who is wriggling, 'Stick your bum out of the window. But remember you're a suffragette when the men come up and give it a kiss.'

'You're making it worse.' Edna wriggles. 'How far's this York place?'

* * * * *

It's twenty-seven miles.

And the sun has risen, as *The Times* promised it would. But only just, behind solid July clouds from here to . . . Macedonia.

It could be winter.

And listen – the Chapel folk are singing 'See Amid The Winter Snow' in their very front carriage.

> 'Now great God to thee we pray
> On our summer holiday
> Go forth with us and abide
> All day long safe by our side.
> Once a year the day comes round!
> Once a year this song shall sound!
> Now be with us as we pray
> Grant to each a happier day.'

* * * * *

36

Flossie's not too happy with his day, in the painters' carriage where Owen reads William Morris in the faint dawn light, Spaldy snores, and Albert waits for his pal's bad temper to pass.

But it isn't passing. Everything is going wrong. Look! When he opens the door and flings an empty Nut Brown bottle at a sheep, he misses, even though the train is only going at sheep speed.

And, even worse, the next beer out of the crate is another India Pale.

Flossie grunts. 'If this was a proper Friday morning, Albie, we'd just be starting on a soapy pint of draught Amber for us breakfasts.'

'Lovely.'

'Free.'

'Aye.'

Flossie wipes his lips with his white silk scarf, plucks off his cap and wipes his head too. 'Think on, Albie. We'd be at brewery now. Me stirring up some more of that green to finish touching up them doors. And you labouring for me, cos old Owensie's still hiding in the dubs reading about his trade unions Mr Holles won't allow him to have, with his trousers round his sandals. And Spaldy's being the chuffing artist again, cleaning out the chuffing brushes again, when they don't need it. Here, what's happening? I can't see!'

* * * * *

Nobody can.

For, with two late whistles, the scarlet locomotive drags the beano into a sudden tunnel. Excursionists squeal and leap to the window to keep out the smoke, and settle back to cuddle and nip each other.

* * * * *

But all is well in the First Class where cocky Mr Atkinson in his blazer is sealed from the world by closed windows and a blind for the sake of his three aunts, who stare at his blonde companion and talk about how much money they are going to be worth to him when they are dead.

Cocky Mr Atkinson! Listen to him whispering to his blonde that the train rhythms are doing her good. And she mustn't be afraid of tunnels! He isn't! And look, he's unpeeling her glove, as she wonders how she will cope when they get to York.

* * * * *

And the train clunks out of the tunnel.

'I'm still blocked buggering solid,' says the ancient blacksmith to Lizzie in their Third Class next-but-one-to-the-front. 'You got a hat pin?'

'It's just a box with me mam's cake and some macaroons for us breakfast, isn't it, Percy?'

But Percy only stares at the colour picture of St Pancras Station, above the mother and her sucking baby.

'You must have some sort of buggering grip,' the blacksmith says.

'I'll feel,' Lizzie says, fingering under her scarf.

* * * * *

Just as Mr Holles in the First Class Lavatory carriage pats the Girl's bum. 'Why are you standing up?'

'Sir, Mrs Holles, sir?'

'Mrs Holles is fortunate enough to have wed me, and therefore to have full use of the one lavatory on the train. Now, she might be a Liberal, but even she is capable so far of using the lavatory on her own. You'll have some brandy.'

'No sir, thank you, sir.'

'Old enough, aren't you?'

'Seventeen, sir.'

'Why do you keep tugging at your skirt?'

'Don't know, sir.'

'I'll be seeing plenty of your legs when we get to the seaside you know.'

Mrs Holles opens the lavatory door and looks in, thinking of that last family holiday. It's so strange how you remember. That lighthouse that hurt her eyes, yes, but – a skeleton? And that run up the grassy hill to some flagpoles that got taller as you ran, and then the bandstand, before you suddenly saw all the wooden pier, stretching right out beyond the waves? Like a bridge!

'Still merely bilious?' Mr Holles says. 'The Girl is now going to recite to us the full details of this morning's hop market as reported in *The Times* and learned by the method I am teaching her.'

The Girl curtsies, and stays standing. 'The hop market, sir, rules quiet and although some growers, sir, have been more accommodating, sir, I think quotation remains virtually unchanged, sir, at six pounds seven shillings and nought pence per hundredweight. And, sir, the general crops outlook, sir, is considered very satisfactory.'

'I consider that very satisfactory too.' Mr Holles pats her bottom. 'I'll buy you a nice present when we stop. We should be nearly there now.'

* * * * *

We should. But nearly where?

The train keeps stopping for points and signals and water and it keeps going backwards.

And everything is so flat – we could be anywhere.

* * * * *

A carpenter's apprentice sees Chesterfield, and leaps up in the middle of the brag game.

'That's what they call their "Crooked Spire".'

'You're in us light, lad.'

But the apprentice is too excited. 'I know why it's crooked! There were this couple who come to get married at Chesterfield. Only, this bride wasn't having a baby. And the spire didn't believe that were possible like, with them getting wed, so he turned round to look at this miracle and he got stuck like it.'

'You'll get stuck if you don't sit down, lad.'

'It were Chesterfield!'

'It were Pontefract where they have lagoons of liquorice to chuck mucky apprentices in!' And they punch theirs out of their light.

* * * * *

'Where exactly are we, Mr Shephard?'

'I would have hazarded more or less Selby, Miss Tidmarsh.'

The loving clerks perched opposite each other, almost knee to knee, in the very middle of their crammed Third Class Smoker have to talk even more softly than in the office where they first met, and whispered about small inconsistencies in certain invoices, seven Christmasses ago.

They have shared all her mint imperials, and smell of them now as they lean into each other, sharing the same breath but not touching.

'I wonder if you could remind us of the guidebook's recommendations for us at York, Mr Shephard?'

'With pleasure. Though the light in here, Miss Tidmarsh . . . with the smoking and er?'

'Please borrow my spectacles, Mr Shephard, they are stronger than yours.' She fumbles, drops them, stands to get them, and squashes her silly hat on the luggage rack as the train jerks. She picks up her spectacles, dusty with tobacco ash and slimy with what might be spit, even though the notice above the picture of the Midland Hotel at Derby prohibits it.

But by now Mr Shephard is reading anyway. 'Here we are. "York County and County Borough ancient Eboracum".'

'I remember "Eboracum" from school!' she says. 'I used to think "Eboracum" sounded so Roman you could almost hear the centurions marching round the walls in their sandals and going off to their hot baths and –'

Mr Shephard frowns round the carriage.

She nods, stares at him with the brown eyes that say 'I have not quite given up'.

He looks back at the book. 'This, er, "Eboracum" of ours is "one-eight-eight northwest London. On River Ouse, of course. Seat of Archbishopric and Minster finest cathedral (Gothic) in England".'

'I've always wanted to see York Minster!'

'Have you? Unfortunately I think we are only allowed ten minutes for the change of locomotive as we transfer to our second railway company in York, Miss Tidmarsh.'

'Never mind!' But her voice is too bright, as if she is going to be giddy again. 'Other people live with disappointment don't they? Though surely there could be something more interesting to look at on long journeys than the Midland Hotel in Derby? And I want my photograph taken today, Mr Shephard.'

'That should not prove to be insuperable as a problem for you, Miss Tidmarsh.'

'And I would like you to be on the photograph with me.'

'How kind, er –' he say softly, and frowns.

She bites her lip and giggles. 'I do hope I am not going to be giddy.'

4

Halfway Up

Holland, Greece and York – Cocky Mr Atkinson and the
blonde – A song for York – The most impressive station in the
kingdom – Mr Wagstaff's surprise present – Poor Mrs Holles
plans an exit – And why the carpenters missed the beano after
Mr Holles got the wind up.

And the beano now rocks and shuffles through Church Fenton, with its four platforms and hanging baskets full of smoky red flowers.

The locomotive stops for water again in a landscape so flat there is a windmill. Has the beano missed York while we dozed? And gone straight on to Holland?

Excursionists stop talking as the locomotive drinks.

And then as we shudder and jolt off again there is a new excitement.

For if you look out of the windows now, you can see thirty shining tracks on both sides of you. And you are skating on them, too fast.

At Holgate Junction a dozen tracks sweep off left.

And the sounds change, as if you have come indoors. The lines split as you rattle over them. And you curve past 'Platform 9'!

There are great Greek columns here, and a fantastical iron roof and a huge blue clock with gold fingers on a fairy-story bridge that floats above the platforms. But you can see none of all this through the smoke from more locomotives champing together here in the early morning than you thought there could be in all England.

What a noise and smell! Rub yourself, and stretch your legs

41

and shake up your liver, disembark before the beano stops, and join the shambles!

* * * * *

Some excursionists do not even bother to disembark for the ten minutes while the scarlet locomotive is swapped for a green one.

Cocky Mr Atkinson's blonde for instance. And cocky Mr Atkinson. She was whispering to him as far back as Church Fenton that she would rather stay with him if the aunts were going to get off to shake up their livers. Specially if he can draw the curtains?

He can, and has done.

And so they sit alone now in their darkened First Class.

'When the aunts die,' he says, 'I am going to be very rich.' And he unpeels her glove.

* * * * *

Albert and Flossie, who will never be rich, have long disembarked and stretched their legs, and are now congering up and down the long platform, kneeling, stretching and swinging their arms as they advance through the morning passengers.

> 'Oh the grand old Duke of York
> He had ten thousand men,
> He marched them up to the top of the hill
> And he marched them down again.'

* * * * *

Miss Tidmarsh and Mr Shephard shrink further into a classical arch as the workpeople advance.

> 'And when they were only halfway up
> They were neither up nor down.'

But once the Duke of York's army has retreated Mr Shephard returns to his guidebook and reads aloud with the book very close to his eyes.

'The station was designed by Thomas Prosser, and completed "as long ago as 1877".'

Miss Tidmarsh says, '1877 is not long ago.'

'Oh?' He peers through a spurt of North Eastern steam. ' "York Station remains one of the grandest and most impres-

42

sive stations in the kingdom." ' He fumbles between his knees. 'I think this other book tells in addition that standing here is reminiscent of standing in the nave of one of the great cathedrals of northern France. Which in a way it is, is it not?'

'I've never seen the great cathedrals of northern France.'

'Nor have I, of course.'

The Duke of York advances and retreats.

She murmurs, 'I am so sorry we cannot talk properly on the train.'

'Yes – er.' He swallows. And wonders if he dare talk properly now? Ask her? Get it over? But he daren't. 'I wonder if you think it might be a good idea to purchase postcards of Mr Prosser's station? We could jot a reassuring message home to your Pa and to Mummy?' He closes the guidebook. 'I am sure tomorrow we shall be allowed to keep the postcards for our own collections. Shall I make a purchase on behalf of – oh. Perhaps not.'

For he has seen Mr Holles in a laughing crowd of Britlings workpeople at the bookstall. He waves Miss Tidmarsh to walk away, down the most impressive station in the kingdom.

And follows her five yards behind, in case anyone notices.

But they don't.

* * * * *

No one's noticing Mr Wagstaff either. He stands now by the steps under the blue and gold clock. The porters have still not brought the table that was clearly arranged and rehearsed more than a month ago.

Ask him how he is – though nobody ever does – and he will say he cannot complain. But he certainly looks peaky. And, in spite of the long leather mackintosh buttoned down to his shoes, he is cold, too. This is because he has been allowed to travel in silence all the way to York in the guard's van, full of Mr Holles's luggage, and on the verandah at the back, in return for a small tip. No doubt he will get pneumonia from it, but at least this year he has not had to watch the shambles.

No one does ask him how he is, here at York, apart from the heavy drinking widow-woman from the Britlings pub by the cemetery at home, who mistakes him for the landlord of the Anchor in Hope by the canal. And does not believe him

43

when he says he is Mr Wagstaff. She says she recognizes his coat, and offers him a drink. But three porters now arrive with a rickety whist table, and Mr Wagstaff rebukes them. They tell him to boil his head, and they do not help him up on to the table.

But listen to him now, shouting through the megaphone at the crowds, not caring that most have no connection with the brewery, beyond drinking as much beer as they can.

'You!' he shouts. 'There are a further six and a half minutes remaining for the exchange of locomotive, after which we shall immediately resume our journey.' He notices Mr Holles's straw hat by the bookstall. But does not turn fast enough. 'There has unfortunately and unnecessarily been some raucousness with windows and other railway appurtenances that do not belong to you, on the first stage of our pilgrimage. Third Class excursionists, and they know to whom I am referring to, have been lucky not to have been seriously maimed as a result of their intemperate behaviour. Excursionists, Britlings insist, must desist from any further interference –'

But someone is poking a rolled newspaper right up inside his buttoned mackintosh, and interfering with him now.

'Got a present for you, Waggy. It's from the bookstall. But it's not a book. Mrs Holles and I don't believe in books, they harbour dust.' Mr Holles hands up an oblong brown paper parcel, and snatches the megaphone.

'Thank you, Mr Holles.'

Excursionists snigger round the whist table. They don't know the joke – but they do know Mr Holles.

Mr Wagstaff knows him too. He carefully pushes the string round the corners of his parcel, and puts it deep in his mackintosh pocket.

Mr Holles shouts, 'It's presents galore today, Waggy. Look what I just bought my Girl. Come on, ducky, let them see your Ingersoll.' He rolls up the maid's sleeve and holds her bare arm and new wristwatch in the air. 'If that's not gold, my cock's a bloater.'

Mr Wagstaff carefully unpeels his brown paper.

'Come on, Waggy. What you got?'

Mr Wagstaff carefully folds the brown paper into his mackintosh pocket and puts a printed sheet of paper between his teeth. And carefully opens his present. It is eight inches of black indiarubber tubing that swells into a fat rubber bulb, with three attachable canvas straps and buckles. He dangles it in one hand and takes the instructions from between his teeth.

'Try it out then, Waggy, whatever it is.'

'Yes, sir.' He slips the instructions into his pocket. He bends to undo the buttons of his long mackintosh, from the ankles to the waist. 'What you have kindly purchased for me, Mr Holles sir, is a gentleman's travelling lavatory. According to the instructions it is strapped to either leg, here or here. I would like to thank you very much indeed, Mr Holles sir. But I shall now have to remove my trousers, if you wish me to demonstrate it more fully.'

Mr Wagstaff turns. Looks at poor Mrs Holles.

And winks at her!

(Doesn't he?)

An insolent, intimate wink that says, 'I know you, Mrs Holles. We are the meek, we are not blessed, for Mr Holles has inherited us. He is our God, bursting in his checked suit with food and drink and so much energy he can burn all our books and strip us naked here just as one day he will kill us in public and still dance and wrestle horses while the crowds applaud.'

Poor Mrs Holles shakes her head. But Mr Wagstaff is not looking at her any more.

(But he did wink, didn't he?)

Poor Mrs Holles turns and pushes away through the crowds that are now applauding.

And Mr Holles grabs Mr Wagstaff's trouser legs, to scramble up on to the whist table. 'Enough of your chuffing about, Mr Wagstaff. We've no desire to see your wedding tackle this early in the morning. All I'll say, as an Anglican, is that God gave it to you, and you've made no use of it, and we all know what Jesus said about burying your talents. But this morning we are more worried about wasps.'

'Wasps, sir?'

'Look here in today's *Times*, man. Page five.' He unrolls *The Times*, smacks it, and opens it out. 'Now we all know you've insured yourself for when you drown us. But what about wasps?'

'Wasps, sir?'

But before Mr Wagstaff can take the paper there is a sudden cold wind that chases up Platform 9. It snatches *The Times's* front and back pages, and as Mr Wagstaff fumbles on the wobbling table, the whole newspaper floats away.

'Look out, man!'

And look out all of us! Watch *The Times* blown apart by the cold winds from Europe.

Most Britlings employees in the crowd know from the Christmas party that Mr Holles can do conjuring tricks. But even they are surprised by this one, for the pages of *The Times* now separate and dance as they ascend into the smoke of Mr Prosser's 1877 roof, and disappear!

What a card Mr Holles is! Smelling of fresh brandy this early in the day! Buying gold watches for plump girl servants in front of his poor wife! And now making newspapers fly above us, to shower the station with philosophy . . .

For look at that *Times*, skipping in and out of the clouds with all our tomorrows in it. Are not tomorrow's racing winners all there already, before the races are even run, if only we know how to look? Everything else that is to come is there too . . . All the coincidences that change our lives are waiting in it just as certainly as the racing winners – and the hours of sunrise and sunset and the times of the tides and history itself, that is already written while we try to live through it.

Look in any old copy of *The Times* newspaper and you can see everything that was going to happen had already started happening . . .

Such earnest thoughts though, at three minutes to six on beano morning!

Mr Holles isn't thinking them. He is whipping Mr Wagstaff with the indiarubber lavatory. 'Shambles! That makes two shambles they've got at York!'

'Sir. There should be no trouble at Scarborough, however, Mr Holles sir. The railway employees there have rehearsed my plan to lock all the exit gates as our Special arrives. The new mayoress will already be waiting on the Welcome rostrum.'

But the wind turns now. And the great crowds on Platform 9 cheer as *The Times* now sinks back down through the smoke. They scatter all down the platform to leap and grab at the separated sheets of the magic newspaper. What a souvenir!

Mr Holles pushes the rubber lavatory into Waggy's megaphone, and blows his whistle.

And sees Mrs Holles. 'And where do you think you are gallivanting off to, Mrs Holles?'

She has only reached the bottom of the stairs to the other platforms where half the trains in England are waiting to take her away.

She stands very still, and old. If she had not stopped to see his conjuring trick . . .

'Come on, Mrs Bilious, you get back in that train.'

He jumps from the table, and blows his whistle again.

* * * * *

And the train leaves a minute early.

The bragging carpenters and their apprentice who saw Chesterfield at Pontefract are still drinking beef tea in the Third Class Refreshment Room, and are left behind.

5

Does This Train Stop at Scarborough?

Romans and scarecrows – The man with the duck eggs – Fun and games in Miss Tidmarsh's carriage – Pass the hat box – Fingers crossed – Conjugals, and what Mr Bardgrave Dean said – How to keep down the population – Where's Bunty? And the North Sea? – A joke – The death of Anne Brontë, the arrival of Donald McGill, and the welcoming new mayoress of Scarborough.

And we're off again!

But best not get too excited. It's still forty-odd miles to the North Sea, even if the new driver and his chuffing green locomotive knows the quickest way. Our train of many colours clunks over the River Ouse as soon as it leaves the great curved station. And at last – if you're facing the sea – on your right you can see the finest Gothic cathedral in England, playing peep-bo through the tall houses.

Wait seven minutes at a level crossing no one ever uses before we set off again. And chuff off into the endless flat lands beyond Eboracum. Miss Tidmarsh's Romans must have got as nostalgic for hills as you are!

The sun is cold behind the clouds on the right, above the sitting cows chewing the pale grass. But what else is there to do after the excitement of York?

Wish you were in another carriage, where all the fun happens?

Tut at all the mucky washing dangling by the track?

Frown at the winding River Derwent that won't decide whether or not it really wants to go to Scarborough?

Or count all the blue and purple flowers and the scarecrows in all the flat fields, where there is nothing to scare?

Or snooze? And have those quick dreams you have on journeys at strange times when your life is being shaken up?

Or you could sing.

* * * * *

Like the jolly Electrical excursionists and their jolly wives are doing. They are now well into their travel medley.

> 'The seats are so small and there's not much to pay
> You sit close together and spoon all the way.
> There's many a Miss will be Missis some day
> Through riding on top of the car!'

* * * * *

Tommy and Spud, the stowaways, ride and snooze.

Monkey is their guard, so that they do not miss the sea. He stands to attention now, with one hand in his pocket, and looks out of the train for the sea, all the long way we've still got till Scarborough.

He is proud to be guard. But he has never seen the sea. So how will he know when it is time to warn Tommy and Spud? Does the sea suddenly ambush you by pouring over the horizon? Or does it seep through the ground and drown you from your feet up?

Monkey holds himself in his torn trouser pocket and waits for the sea to surprise him.

There were three men, two wives and a daughter connected with Retail who travelled with them to York. But there are only the stowaways now, and the man with the duck eggs that he keeps shelling into his paper bag, and slowly chewing with his eyes shut.

Tommy grunts in his snooze, and thinks his way through all the books of the Old Testament. He is right, too, except for getting Joel and Hosea arse-abouts first time through.

When Monkey dribbles, Spud kicks him in the ankle and says, 'Going to kill you.'

The duck eggs smell horrible.

* * * * *

'Shitsharks!'

The Third Class Smokers shriek and clap.

Miss Tidmarsh and Mr Shephard flinch. They now sit side

49

by side with their backs to the engine, because the Third Class Smokers have swapped seats after York to play cards with a pack they stole from the station bookstall.

Miss Tidmarsh and Mr Shephard dare not talk at all now, for the Smokers' game has sudden silences. They pretend to snooze, upright and separate. But each time the card game gets exciting, or the train lurches, they are pushed into each other. And each time they murmur apologies, as if they do not really know each other.

The Smokers assume Miss Tidmarsh and Mr Shephard are just another tired married couple having a glum beano together. They are not, after all, young, and they do not touch or talk, do they? And Miss Tidmarsh *is* wearing a wedding ring under her glove!

'Shitsharks!'

* * * * *

Percy and Lizzie aren't touching or talking either.

Or Percy isn't. He sits scowling because Bunty wasn't on the platform at York, eleven miles back . . . all lemon hair and love, running through the train smoke to him and saying, 'I will, I will!'

'It wants eating up,' Lizzie says, lifting the top of her hat box and nibbling.

The mother is still feeding her toothy baby, and the ancient blacksmith is still struggling with his blocked pipe. He has rolled up a strip of newspaper he found at York round Lizzie's hairgrip, which he is teasing into the bottom of his pipe bowl. 'Bugger isn't it.'

There are six extra excursionists in the middle, since York. They frown about Retail and children nowadays and eggs.

Five miles nearer the sea, Lizzie offers Percy a macaroon.

He scowls.

She offers the hat box round the carriage. The Retail people shake their heads. But the blacksmith claws a handful of cake into his mouth and chews, between blowings down his pipe to get the newspaper out again. And the mother squeezes a palmful of cake into her baby. And flops back smiling. Though she leaves her dress undone. 'Never stop do they, bless them.'

Percy scowls.

Lizzie sticks out her tongue with macaroon all over it. 'Give us a kiss, you, it's the beano.'

* * * * *

Mr Holles gnaws a beano chicken from the Midland Railways gift hamper, and tells the Girl of his charitable plan to set up a strictly disciplined school for orphaned females.

* * * * *

But look there!

Quick!

It's not Scarborough – but it *is* a white horse in that field!

> 'Whitehorsewhitehorsegivemegoodluck
> Whitehorsewhitehorsegivemegoodluck
> Whitehorsewhitehorsegivemegoodluck'

You can almost hear the sound of crossing fingers all down the train as we wait to go under a bridge.

Even in the front carriage, where the singing Chapel people have too much to believe already, one contralto and one tenor look at each other for a brief moment, and secretly chant, and cross their fingers behind Hymn 277:

> 'O Beulah land, sweet Beulah land,
> As on thy highest mount I stand.'

* * * * *

Two flat miles on there is a small bridge with a magpie on it. Fingers are uncrossed. Now we only have to look for magpies.

* * * * *

But in the Ladies Only the suffragettes resume their reading. For pages one, two, twenty-three and twenty-four of Mr Holles's lost newspaper from York have ended up with Bess, Edna and Ada from Washing. They are catching up on the news from the law courts.

'Go on reading, Bess love. You're the only one of us what can do it right.' Edna sits clutching her knees like a child in a nursery waiting to be told the wonderful story of Little Black Sambo all over again.

'You only want it cos it's all about men.'

'Yes.'

'Your trouble is you are cock-struck.'

'Yes.'

'And you always were.' But Ada sits back to listen, too. 'Now we've sorted that out, off you go again, Bess.'

Bess points her finger at each word as she reads. A lot of them are new since she was at school. ' "Mr Justice Bardgrave Dean pronounced a decree of restitution of conjugal rights on the petition of Mrs Alice Crawshaw-Williams against her husband." '

Edna squeezes her knees. 'Another conjugal! Ow, Ada.'

'It's all them law courts do down London.'

'I know,' Edna clutches herself. 'They're right mucky. You should have heard what my father used to tell us about Prince Edward before he became the Peacemaker, bless him.' And then, 'And before he died, of course.'

Bess reads slowly. ' "The marriage was a happy one until the respondent, Mr Crawshaw-Williams, developed an affection for another lady." '

' "Developed an affection", eh? Ow, Ada.'

' "He was cited as co-respondent. A restoration of conjugal rights to be obeyed by the respondent within fourteen days." '

Edna clutches herself. 'Fourteen nights more like. "I'm asleep." "Sorry love, judge's orders." Eh? Come on then, Bess, finish it off!'

'No,' Bess says. 'Pages are hurting me fingers. Here.' And she pushes it at Edna.

'You know I can't read print fast enough for it to make sense.'

Ada says, 'Shouldn't have spent your schooldays chasing lads then.'

'Ow, Ada, leave us some hair.'

A ruined monastery pokes up beyond the river on the left. 'It's a funny way of treating women, all that,' says Ada. 'And you can stop relishing it, Edna, we're suffrag-chuffing-ettes today.'

And the monastery slides back towards York.

* * * * *

Not long to the seaside now, surely?

Look out and sniff for the ozone. Oh we would like to be beside the seaside!

52

The beano will be happening without us if we don't hurry.

*   *   *   *   *

And five carriages back from the suffragettes there is another discussion.

'Just listen to what I'm saying, Owensie. It's the only way they've got of keeping down their population.'

'Flossie the –'

'I thought you'd have something to say about the population, Owensie. What with your "free love" and your widow woman.'

'It's rubbish, Flossie, and –'

'And it's you what spouts it.'

The debate adjourns as Flossie stabs the cork in the very last bottle. Five miles southwest of Malton he succeeds. 'Chuffing India Ale again.' He gives Albie first drink. 'My missis said I should have married Albert instead of her, you know.'

Owen nods. 'And why shouldn't you? Male comradeships might well prove to be the model for relationships in the future when we are all free. We had a visiting speaker at the Clarion.'

'Politics is it, Owensie?'

'Of course.'

'No thanks.'

Three miles pass. But we're still not there. Spaldy rubs his eyes.

Owen says, 'It's obvious when –'

'All I'm saying, Owensie, is population's getting too big. Albert read us out that bit of that newspaper what I caught him at York with him being my pal. Got his own views on that mind you, haven't you, Albie?'

'I have. They won't dare use ships and guns they've got nowadays, they're that new. We've not had a real war for years, have we?'

Flossie wipes the bottle on his white scarf and passes it to Albert. 'A point there, eh Owensie? A wrong one but it is a point. I say they've got their ships and guns and so they'll have to use them, whoops.'

And woody hills leap up on both sides of the carriage. Thick yellow smoke caught by the sudden valley rolls in through the open window, and tastes of burnt Yorkshire pudding.

The debate adjourns while they cough.

Owen recovers first. 'The working classes of Europe aren't going to be fooled by newspapers like that one Albert's got there. We know who owns the newspapers, don't we?'

'No.'

'And why war suits them?'

'No.'

'There'll be general strikes all over Europe.' But he coughs again. And his words dangle like smuts.

Flossie opens the door and chucks the last, empty bottle into the smoke. 'How are general strikes reckoned to help?'

'The train drivers won't drive the trains to the war.'

'Soldiers'll drive them.'

'The soldiers themselves will be on strike all over Europe. We've no quarrel with the workers of Russia and Germany, have we? The workers – '

'I'm a worker, Owensie.'

'Yes, and there are more of us than – '

'I'll fight for my country. Fact, I'll be first.'

Albert nods. 'We all will. And the trouble is, Owensie, we don't know owt about what we're saying, do we? It's just summat to talk about to while away time like, while we get there.'

Flossie says, 'I know what I know, Owensie.' He bends over and breaks wind. His cap falls off.

Albert dashes to the window. 'We're being gassed! Get your windows open!'

The train chunters out beyond the woody hills now and turns sharp left. And by chance Albert sees straight into the Chapel party's carriage, and shouts to them. 'Help! Watch out you lot! Flossie's started blowing off!'

* * * * *

But the Chapel party now are singing of cool Siloam's Shady Rill, Sharon's Dewy Rose. And they cannot hear the warning.

* * * * *

Nor can Percy, staring out of his half-open window as the train yanks left.

But he can suddenly see into the First Class.

54

But Bunty won't be in there, will she? He sees Mr Holles standing up, dancing with his maid. The curtains are shut in the one next to it.

Percy scowls and heaves the strap to bang the window shut, but it crashes open and he will spend the rest of the journey trying to mend it, while the Retail people tut, the mother feeds, and the blacksmith pokes at the newspaper still blocking his pipe. 'Buggering pipes.'

* * * * *

Yes, but where is the sea?

Lean right out, like more and more excursionists are doing each slow half-mile. Risk having your head sliced off and carried back to York by the oncoming train. Why aren't there some people? Why is everything so flat? If the driver's got lost, shouldn't someone do something?

* * * * *

And Flossie snorts at Owen. 'Just study some history.'

'Whose history?'

'History! What happened.'

'What happened depends on who writes it. And who they write about as well, Flossie. And who for. We've even had our pasts stolen from us. We've – '

'Whoops!'

'Give over, Flossie,' Albert yelps. 'We're being gassed again.'

'Have to admit it, Albie,' Flossie admits. 'It's Owensie's fault, mind you. I warned him we didn't want his politics today.'

Albert gasps. 'You'll have to stop, Owensie.'

'You won't listen!' Owen says.

Flossie shrugs. 'Not having your politics spoiling us beano, told you.'

'Their politics spoil your life.'

'Tripe. And you think we're tripe, all on us, trying to make something of us lives.'

'What about Spaldy's eyes? And you drink too much. Why?'

'Chuff off talking.'

'It shouldn't make you miserable talking and having to think, Flossie. We can change things by what we talk and think.'

55

'Go home to your widow and give her one, get it out of your system.'

'It's not my system, is it?'

'Tripe.'

A slow flat mile further on Spaldy stands up at the window. 'I hope we get some sunshine. You get colours to paint by that sea what we never get at home.'

'Aye,' Albert says. He is tearing *The Times* into careful quarters and folding them into a thick wad in his back pocket. 'We'll need these if last year is owt to go by.'

Flossie says, 'There's always his political leaflets for that. Up the workers, eh Owensie?'

* * * * *

The train judders, stops, hisses, clanks, has a drink.

'We're there!'

We're not. But there is a joke to help, passed up the train by each excursionist who leans out of the window to get first look at the sea. It gets as far as the very front, where the Chapel party are packing up the hymn books into a scratched-out Britlings crate.

The Chapel folk smile as well. Allelujah!

'Excuse me, driver,' the joke goes, 'but does this train stop at Scarborough?'

'I hope so, sir, or we shall all end up in the North Sea.'

* * * * *

But where *is* the North Sea?

The jolly Electricians and their jolly wives are running out of songs.

The train judders and starts again. The excursionists are silent in case the driver thinks they are getting too excited.

* * * * *

And Seamer West signal box slides very slowly past on your left.

There is a chill now, when you poke out.

(Did you ever see another magpie? Shouldn't you have?)

We must be nearly there. Look – a goat in that field. That looks like a Scarborough goat.

And those five cows – sitting down. That must mean something?

Look – a gas works. Three red-brick chapels with steeples.

A road of red-brick terraces just like home. Only clean.

There's still no sea, tidal, waving or gushing. But we are there. Look, we're sliding on to a platform. And it says SCARB in chalk by that trolley of brown-paper parcels.

And the chuffing train's squeaking. And hurting your teeth.

Mind you, we'll only have just about enough time to buy a stick of rock and we'll have to be back on Platform 2 to go home. But we are chuffing here!

Alle-chuffing-lujah!

* * * * *

Scarborough's porters run for cover.

'All change!'

'All change!'

Owen nods at that. There's hope everywhere if you listen.

* * * * *

And the Britlings Beano Special slithers down Platform 1 all grimy green engine and even muckier scarlet coaches that have done the whole long journey.

Doors smack open, excursionists fall out and limp down the platform. Even Mr Wagstaff, icy after his journey in the guard's van, disembarks illegally before his own announcement that the train has arrived, and begins to run in his long raincoat down the platform to the table by the locked exit gates.

But the exit gates have not been locked in spite of all the rehearsals. Mr Wagstaff is punched in the kidney, kicked twice on the knee, and carried along in the pushing crowds.

'Britlings people,' he shouts. 'The exits are all closed. In the light of our post-mortem after Rhyl – '

But no one can hear Mr Wagstaff, not even Mr Wagstaff himself.

What should happen next is very clear from the Illustrative Programme. A speech of gratitude to God. A non-sectarian prayer. A short address to and from the new mayoress of Scarborough. Presentations. Reminders re first aid, insurance, sensible eating and return times.

But none of it will happen next, of course.

It's a shambles.

* * * * *

'It's a shambles. Let me get at Wagstaff,' Mr Holles calls. He smacks the Girl. He leans out of the First Class and beckons a purple clogger with three black teeth who is breasting through the crowds.

* * * * *

Mr Shephard and Miss Tidmarsh shelter from the shambling crowds by crushing themselves against a red-and-gold chocolate machine. (Though they still manage not to touch.)

Miss Tidmarsh pulls at her ruined silly hat and calculates that two-ninths of the beano are already over, if you count the journeys.

Mr Shephard consults the book. ' "Scarborough, Yorks. North East England. On coast. Queen of the Watering Places. Population 33,776." And Anne Brontë came here to recuperate, when she was dying of consumption, Miss Tidmarsh.'

'Did she?'

'You sound doubtful, Miss Tidmarsh? It is written here. Look.'

'No – sorry. I mean, did she recuperate?'

'Oh, sorry . . . She did die of course because she is buried at St Mary's Church. But whether or not she died after she recuperated . . .'

He looks over the top of the chocolate machine and wonders if he dare ask her, here, now. Before the day is ruined?

* * * * *

Donald McGill, the seaside postcard man, will soon be coming asking questions in Scarborough too, as uninvited as the Britlings family. But no Chapel folk will ever laugh at his seaside jokes.

'Hello, old man, are you recuperating?'

'Oh no, old chap. I'm much to ill for that sort of thing.'

* * * * *

Mr Shephard dares not ask Miss Tidmarsh his question. For the crowds suddenly move again, and Miss Tidmarsh is pushed away as the brewery corkscrews and bottlenecks through the exits, and explodes all over Scarborough.

There are two minutes of raucousness and shambles.

* * * * *

Mr Wagstaff is still apologizing to the mayoress when Mr Holles arrives through the last of the pushing crowds. He rides on the shoulders of the purple clogger with three black teeth who now puts him gently on the table and wishes him many more such days.

Mr Wagstaff introduces the new mayoress. Mr Holles helps her on to the table and kisses her coat of arms with the chains nuzzling her breast. 'You'll have to excuse the shambles, my dear. This is a Waggy excursion. Many deaths so far, Waggy?'

'No, sir. Do you wish to make your speech now, Mr Holles? I'm afraid the locomotive's lackadaisical approach to the platform rather allowed the excursionists to – '

'I don't make no speeches with nobody listening, Waggy. That's what you do.' He puts his arm round the mayoress. 'It's the same sort of raggety business we had at Rhyl, and there were deaths by lunchtime there.' He squeezes the mayoress's chain, nipping the skin on her shoulder. She squeals.

'And there is the matter of my dip at eleven, and the insurance, Waggy.'

'Thank you for reminding me, sir.' And Mr Wagstaff shouts down the megaphone, 'Britlings employees are reminded that the return journey will commence at six forty p.m. and that until then you are insured to a total of a hundred pounds in case of death, two pounds per week for a total disability if it can be proved that no negligence – '

'Wasps, Waggy!'

'Oh yes, sir. Yes. Mr Holles thoughtfully drew our attention to wasps at York. I have given the matter some thought. My *prima facie* rule of thumb on wasps, sir, is that wasps I assume to be covered by the insurance kindly taken out by Britlings, provided no personal carelessness is involved and no encouragement has been given to the wasps in any way.'

But Mr Holles is now kissing the new mayoress on the mouth. 'It must be the ozone, my dear. I'm a married man normally. The first Mrs Holles is a Liberal, as you must have guessed from the fact that she is still cowering in the First Class in case she meets the workpeople. Go fetch her, Waggy!'

'Sir – your dip at eleven?'

But Mr Holles is kissing the mayoress, nipping her shoulders again, and shouting, 'Do I taste of brandy, your highness?'

The new mayoress shakes her chain, and welcomes him, the other shareholders, the agencies, the dear friends and families and the workpeople.

Mr Holles kisses her a last time and twirls her daintily round the table.

* * * * *

Mr Shephard and Miss Tidmarsh walk down the platform five yards apart.

* * * * *

And cocky Mr Atkinson offers his hand to help his aunts descend from the First Class. But he lifts the blonde by her warm waist.

She apologizes for having felt so faint, and for having to sit waiting in the carriage so long since the arrival, until the platform was quite clear. She apologizes for not being able to mix with crowds.

* * * * *

And Mr Wagstaff delivers poor Mrs Holles and the Girl to the table by the exit.

Mr Holles says, 'We're just off for a bracing ride on the toast rack along the sea front with the new mayoress here, Mrs Holles. That should shake up your biliousness. Waggy will see our luggage to the Grand.' He clutches the new mayoress to his checked waistcoat. 'You're a very regal person, mayoress. But do you know about Queen Augusta Victoria's hospital operation yesterday? Thought not. I've a remarkable memory, unlike some people who can't even remember which one Augusta Victoria is. I'll tell you all about it.'

And he does, as he sweeps his three women off to the tram car.

It is four and a half minutes since the beano arrived. Platform 1 is empty. And you can hear the seagulls laughing on the station roof.

* * * * *

The fuzzy beano photograph will be taken on Platform 2, here, tonight.

We know Mr Holles will be on it, of course, standing on the table in the middle staring at some sudden unthinkable future he has just glimpsed. And poor Mrs Holles will be smiling next to him. And Mr Wagstaff will be cheerful. And it is, of course, the purple clogger who will be pointing to his mouth, though you cannot see his three teeth on the photograph.

And those railway workers who are hiding now will be on the front rows in their uniforms, terrified.

But some people we now know to be actually arrived here at Scarborough won't be on the picture tonight. Mr Atkinson and his aunts and the blonde for example? And Owen? And the suffragettes?

Still, that's tonight when it's all over. We've only just got here. We might as well at least have a look at Scarborough first, if some of us have come all this way to be drowned. (Like we were at Rhyl.)

PART THREE

6

Beside the Seaside

The painters cry – Mr Shephard changes his mind, and he and
Miss Tidmarsh decide not to swim – Tommy teaches the
stowaways to beg – The Scotch fishergirls – Anne Brontë
again, and what Lizzie does to her – What history teaches –
The view from the Castle – Mr Holles explains Jesus to
Monkey, who witnesses a miracle – A hymn to the North Sea.

It's three minutes past eight now.

And the four Britlings painters are already staring at the
grey sea from South Sands, and crying in the grey wind. The
last three early-morning bathers are trotting back up the
beach to their hotels for breakfasts.

'It just goes on and on, Albie.'

'Aye, Floss. It's vast.'

Spaldy thumbs tobacco chunks into his pipe, without
looking down. 'When folk paint it, they make it blue.'

'Aye, Spaldy.'

'It's not blue.'

And Albert recites, ' "The sea is calm tonight. The tide is
full." ' He opens his legs, joins his hands behind his back,
lifts his chin and proceeds: ' "The cliffs of England stand
something and vast out in the tranquil bay. Come to the
window!" '

'It's poetry,' says Flossie. 'He were the best poetry reciter in
our school, my Albert. All but thirty year ago.'

' "You hear the grating roar of pebbles what the waves
draw back and fling." '

'Aye, that's it.'

' "Pebbles what the waves draw back and fling at their

something up the high sand, strand, begin and cease and then again begin." ' He frowns. ' "With tremendous something slow, and bring the eternal note of sadness in." '

They listen for the sadness. Gulls shriek all the way to the white lighthouse at the harbour on their left. Fifty-three Scotch fishergirls slice herrings and sing of home.

Flossie says, 'You're saying nowt for once, with your red tie flapping, Owensie?'

'It's bound to make you think, Flossie.'

'I know what you're thinking, mind you.'

'Do you?' Owen asks, for he is thinking of Mrs E. and oatcakes.

'The working class of Europe only gets to see this once a year. While them bosses sup brandy in that Grand Hotel behind us all summer, and didn't need a holiday in the first place.'

Owen grins. 'Sounds as if you're catching it, brother.'

'I don't need to. There's nothing wrong with me, see, Owensie.'

And Albert recites, ' "With tremendous cadence" *Cadence*! That's the one. It's all coming back, Floss.'

'Aye, and you deserve it, too.'

They listen again.

Scarborough is grey, from the Norman castle on the crumbling cliff that splits the bays, to the bubbling spa water just going on sale at the Spa on their left, at a ha'penny draught or a penny with grey bubbles.

Spaldy wipes his eyes. 'I'm off while there's still some sea left.'

'Chose what you're painting?'

'I'm off up that castle. Where'll you be round six?'

'Nearest pub you can get Britlings at, by that harbour.'

Spaldy picks up his paints.

Owen says, 'I must be off, too.'

'Aye, you go and tell folks how wonderful us workers are.'

Aye Floss, I will.' And the landscape painter and the revolutionary turn and walk up the shiny flat beach. When the artist stumbles, the revolutionary holds his arm.

'Tha's shivering, Albie, what's up?'

'Someone walking over us grave, Flossie.'

66

Flossie puts his arm over his little pal's shoulder. 'There's a pub somewhere in Scarborough where they give you oysters and tripe and you only have to buy your own stout.'

They turn, wiping their eyes.

A tram sings along the front past the Seawater Hospital and goes suddenly inland under a bridge. The new mayoress and her complementary party are the only passengers on the open top deck.

Flossie looks up from the tram to the bridge and yells, 'Here Albie! See them? They are from Britlings. It's that snotty pair from Accounts.' And he shouts up the empty beach. 'Get capurtling, you two. You haven't got all day.'

* * * * *

And the snotty pair from Accounts shrink behind the Cliff Bridge toll booth.

'Oh dear, Trevor.'

'Yes, er.' Mr Shephard peers in at the small window. 'Excuse me? Er, sorry.'

'Bridge or Spa?' says a young voice from the dark.

'I think just the bridge for now, please. I think we did choose, Miss Tidmarsh, the afternoon session on the Spa, listening to the afternoon concert and taking the waters and so on, didn't we?'

'Bridge is a ha'penny,' says the young voice.

'Ah yes, thank you.' Mr Shephard unbuttons his purse. He has nothing less than a shilling. The seagulls zoom on to the Cliff Bridge (which dates from 1826 and forms the principal entrance to the Spa, as Mr Shephard well knows from the guidebooks).

'Each,' the young voice adds.

Miss Tidmarsh holds out her purse. 'Please, Mr Shephard?' She pushes it at him. It falls on to the pavement, spilling coins and tram tickets. 'Sorry.' She bends and rips her left stocking at the knee. And begins shaking again.

'That's quite all right, Miss Tidmarsh,' Mr Shephard says. And to the young voice in the dark he says, 'A ha'penny each, wasn't it? Two please.' He pushes the shilling coin through the window.

'Can't do it. I'm not a bank. This is the bridge to the Spa.'

Mr Shephard knows all about that, too. And that the Spa

was once the Spaw. That there are two spa-water wells – the northern one richer in sulphate of magnesium and the other in chalybeate. (Though it used to be the other way round.) The great Spa repairs of 1876 cost £70,000. The Spa Grand Hall seats 3,000. There are promenades, shops and a café, billiard room and photographer. The new open-air bandstand features two entirely different daily concerts by Mr Alick Maclean's Orchestra, and it includes, this afternoon, the celebrated German cornet player Herr Vincent Bach essaying Sir Arthur Sullivan's 'The Lost Chord'.

Mr Shephard, however, says none of what he knows.

Instead he says, 'I think perhaps we will come back later.' And he takes back his shilling.

They walk from the toll booth to the iron fencing over the Valley Road.

'Trevor?' Miss Tidmarsh says. She notices that he is shaking like she is. 'I do wonder if it might not be better if you took my purse?'

'Of course, yes. Certainly. Of course. The only problem would seem to be the workpeople.' But she pushes her purse down into his pocket.

He frowns through the railings and then back at the guidebook. 'Yes, now down there is the Rotunda Museum, with its famous skeleton. And that should be the main entrance to the Aquarium, yes there it is. "A Moorish extravaganza capable of accommodating ten thousand. Now the so-called 'Fun Palace' or 'Scarborough's Umbrella'." Constructed in, let me see, "1886 and no longer used as an aquarium as such, but specializing in", here we are, "entertainment for sixpence. Its side shows this year include the Amazing Electrical Lady and the Bicycling Martinies. There's also a Hall of Laughter and an Egyptian Hall with illusionists." All for sixpence, Miss Tidmarsh.'

Sixpence each! To be alone together under the umbrella all day. Nobody would notice him down there among the Electric Ladies and Moorish Extravaganzas. He could ask his question down there. But he is already speaking. 'No, I don't think the People's Palace is exactly us. It does also have, I notice, a free dance floor among the Moorish Extravaganza serviced by an efficient orchestra . . . No, I certainly don't think so. Do you?'

They do not look at each other.

'We can still go across the toll bridge now if you really – though I did find the young man was quite – '

'Quite, Trevor,' she reassures him. And adds, 'Doesn't the sea look cold?'

'Yes, I must say I don't think I shall be swimming today.'

'Do you swim, Trevor?'

'No, I'm afraid not. Do you?'

'No.' And she adds, 'Of course not.'

* * * * *

Tommy is ten yards up the hill, teaching the other stowaways how to beg, as they all sit on the bars of the grates of the Grand Hotel. Warm breakfasts breathe out over them.

'I'm starving, me,' Monkey says.

'You're mental more like,' Spud says.

Tommy says, 'We'll get some snap when we've got some brass. We reckon to be rehearsing.'

And they rehearse. 'Inasmuch-as-ye-have-done-it-unto-one-of-these-my-little-ones-you-do-it-unto-me-amen!'

Spud says, 'Bet you was learned that at Primitive Methodists with old Waggy.'

'Weren't.'

'Before you bust that window.'

'Didn't.'

'My mum says you've got religion on your brain.'

'I only go for the outings and the books,' Tommy says. He looks up at the grey Scarborough sky and adds, 'and bleeding Jesus, course.'

They continue their rehearsal.

> 'Pity the children of the poor
> Who never pick the daisies . . .
> They need a holiday ye rich
> May God reward the giver. Amen.'

Tommy says, 'What you do now, you lift your hand up like this at the mester, but you keep staring at the missis.'

'Yeah, Tommy.' And they rehearse that too.

Tommy says, 'But we'll get down that sea first, and wesh us faces.'

Spud says, 'I've not come here to wesh me face.'

69

But Monkey yells, 'Yeah, Tommy. I never see the sea, me, wait!'

And Tommy's already racing towards it, through a fret of bacon and toast and coffee, yelling

> 'Clean hands and face and tidy hair
> Are better than fine clothes to wear.'

* * * * *

Mr Holles in the finest clothes of all the beano is down the harbour with his three women.

Behind them, scores of trippers sit shivering on the wall, to watch the bare-armed Scotch fishergirls bending over great barrels of herring, with their bandaged hands slicing and spurting themselves and the grey morning with blood and insides.

The stench is remarkable.

'Wonderful workers!' Mr Holles shouts to the new mayoress. 'Take note, Mrs Holles.'

But Mrs Holles is remembering her father, the bright lighthouse, the skeleton and the long wooden pier. There *is* a lighthouse here, though it's smaller than it was, and not so bright. There is no skeleton, but you don't expect skeletons to stay for ever. But where is the wooden pier, sticking right out beyond the flagpost and bandstand and little hills that they ran up? She cut her knee that day, of course, at the end of that wooden pier. That was why Father had had to carry her, and why there was blood on his waistcoat, when he pretended mother would be angry with him, and . . . But the 'piers' here at the harbour are all stone, and merely circle the boats.

'Much appreciate all this, your highness.' Mr Holles yells at the new mayoress. 'Glad you showed me these Scotch lasses in spite of their smell. They're just what I need at the brewery. You can invite them back on my train tonight, and we'll leave our so-called trades unionites here with you, eh?'

The Scotch girls do not look up from their bloody work even now when Mr Holles yells that he has heard, mind you, that they double their wages by whoring in Whitby by night.

'It might account for their smell, mayoress,' he confides. 'But now you must show us your museum. There's something rather clever in there Mrs Holles wants to see.'

* * * * *

'You want to eat it, Percy.'

'I hate your mother's cake.'

The golden hand of the black clock up at St Mary's church clonks over to nine o'clock. It's draughtier up here than anywhere in the whole South Bay that St Mary's has watched over for seven centuries. It's always cold on this Yorkshire hillside where Anne Brontë lies dead under a graveful of red flowers. For, recuperated or not, she died aged 29, though the stonemason was not sure either.

Lizzie sits in the red flowers, with her back to the gravestone.

'I hate your mother, too,' Percy says, lobbing cake at the seagulls' beaks.

'You might as well eat it, then I won't have to cart it about.'

'I'll shove it somewhere in a minute.'

'Can if you want.'

And he stops lobbing cake for a moment.

Lizzie sniggers and slides down the gravestone to lie flat on the red flowers. She closes her eyes. 'More like a wedding bed than a grave, this.'

And she rolls on to her tummy and goes to sleep. She cannot tell for how long because Anne Brontë's windy grave is one of the few places in South Bay where you can't see St Mary's clonking out your short life in large Roman numerals. And she dreams in her sleep however long it is, and that filthy dream includes Percy talking about Bunty. 'What she's done, is to get round the station mester and come on a later service train. She'll be running up and down that platform looking for me now while I'm stuck up here in a chuffing graveyard with you and your cake and all these chuffing seagulls. What you brought me up here for, anyway?'

Lizzie opens her eyes. 'She's not coming, Perce.'

'Bunty calls me Perce when we're on us own.'

'I know.'

'You know too much.'

'I know what you wanted her to do Good Friday.'

Lizzie hudges up the gravestone and stares at Percy.

'Christ!'

71

'What's up now, Perce?'

'I've left me cloth on that train.'

'It don't look like you'll be needing it now.'

'Me mam'll kill me when she goes in our front room at Christmas.'

Lizzie turns and fingers the letters of the gravestone. The north winds blow. 'No bloke's ever pinched his mother's tablecloth for me, Perce.'

'You're not Bunty.'

'What's so special about Bunty's arse that she can't get it wet then?'

And then, ' "Here lie the remains of Anne Brontë, daughter of Rev. P. Brontë, incum-summat of Howarth, Yorkshire. She died aged twenty-eight, May 28 1849." '

If you want, you can sense the Brontë sisters up here with you this wuthering morning. And they can be a comfort sometimes to plain Yorkshire couples tragically together in the northwinds.

'Fancy coming here out of the wind, Percy?'

He doesn't.

Lizzie says, 'Fancy being dead at twenty-eight then? We're not far off that ourselves.'

He hurts his neck on his collar as he throws all the cake he has left at the chubbiest seagull in Scarborough laughing at him from the toe-end of Anne Brontë.

It squawks off and hovers above the church, not sure where it should go.

* * * * *

If the chubby gull decides to fly down towards the Spa it will find Mr Holles kissing the new mayoress outside the Rotunda Museum. 'Thank you, your highness. Well worth the sixpence to those who have to pay. Your old ducking stool for dipping scolding women in the sea was also most historical.'

The new mayoress thanks him for his interest, and for the brewery's kindness in choosing Scarborough for their outing. But she really must leave him now owing to the pressure of other engagements. And indeed she has missed three already, while travelling early-morning Scarborough with this energetic brewer and his women.

'See you on the platform tonight, your majesty.' She is

kissed again, and leaves unsteadily by the tram lift to the Grand Hotel. From there she walks towards the new town hall, but she stands in the town hall gardens for some moments by the disturbing statue of Queen Victoria (looking far younger than she ever was), shaking and saying, 'Oh dear, what an energetic man!'

Meanwhile, poor Mrs Holles is shivering in the wind that lashes under Cliff Bridge on its way inland to get warm.

An energetic Mr Holles is poking the Girl with a large postcard of the Rotunda Museum. 'Marvellous what you can learn from history.'

* * * * *

This morning in history is getting chillier. The grey wind that blows straight in off the sea comes all the way from Copenhagen, Riga – Moscow even.

The clouds are so low now, you cannot tell whereabouts in the sky the beano sun is hiding.

It is an irritable morning. It will be easier if it rains. We can go inside then, instead of shivering out here doing ourselves good.

* * * * *

If the chubbiest seagull from Anne Brontë's grave flies upwards it will find Spaldy the painter inside the castle walls. Watching a boy in a sailor suit playing with a slot telescope, and tormenting his shivering nanny.

Spaldy's painting stuff is unpacked on the grass. Squeezed paint tubes. Easel. Stained palette. Brushes, turps, four rags. But his one canvas is still parcelled up in overlapping layers of brown paper sealed with red wax.

There is so much to paint and only one canvas and one day.

* * * * *

'Mester?'

Mr Holles, in the tram queue now, peers down over his checked stomach at a bristly head. 'Talking to me, lad?'

'Inasmuch-as-you-have-done-what-you-done-you-done-it-to-the-little-ones-amen, mester. Lend's a penny, mester?'

'Don't yaffle. I like lads to look at me when they're talking to me.'

'You're hurting my ear, mester.'

73

'Begging is against the by-laws by the foreshore.' Mr Holles drops on one knee.

The queue gathers round to stare. You don't miss free entertainment at the seaside.

'What's your name, son?'

'Monkey. And please, mester, I've never seen the sea afore. And I've lost me dad.'

Mr Holles nods. 'I have lost many things myself, Monkey. And I have many regrets.' He looks up at Mrs Holles. And then back at Monkey. He takes a penny from his pocket.

'Amen, mester.'

'What will you do with it?'

'Spend it, mester.'

'On what?'

'Spice, mester.'

'You will not look for someone worse off than yourself to give it to?'

Monkey stares.

Mr Holles puts the penny back in his pocket. 'So you do not believe in charity, either.'

'You've got to, mester. Jesus says.'

'Jesus does not say so.'

'Tommy says Jesus says so.'

'Tommy is wrong. I am elected church warden at St Lukes which is the most prosperous church on my side of town. We send baskets of money to stop the niggers eating each other. If Jesus did indeed say what you and Tommy say, he says my church would be empty. Ah no, but you'll say Jesus did overturn the money tables, didn't he? I'll say yes, but for a start it wasn't his own money he turned over. And Jesus was interested in sin. That's why he gave up the honest, fairly unprofitable trade of carpentry.' The crowd murmurs. 'We are all sinners is what Jesus said. And one day we'll all be invoiced for our sins. Now you'll say to me, but you're a rich man, Mr Holles, and a fat one, you'll never get through the eye of a needle. I'll reply, correct, and since I have more sins and more avoirdupois than you because I have more pennies, I shall need more forgiveness than you, and that's why I am a more regular churchgoer than you. And why, in turn, I know more about it all than you, and would be grateful if you'll pray for me.'

There is a crackling on the tram wires. Mr Holles stands up.

Monkey calls, 'I did me poem. I want me penny, mester.'

Mr Holles says, 'Poor Mrs Holles did poems before she married me. She will confirm that they don't work.' And then, 'All aboard!'

He ushers his women on to the tram. The queue lets him pass, shuffles and discusses the many meanings of the free entertainment they have just enjoyed that has now just finished.

Or nearly finished.

For Monkey now spots a penny on the pavement where Mrs Holles and the Girl were standing.

A real penny.

He stamps on it and looks up at the grey sky until the tram has sung off up Valley Road.

And who dropped Monkey's penny?

Monkey strokes it, bites it, presses it. It is real. Monkey decides it was Jesus. He runs back along the front to the Tepid Seawater Baths where Tommy promised he'd wait.

* * * * *

It is twenty-five past ten now.

The sea has slipped so far out there is only half an inch of horizon for the *Cambria* steamboat to puff on.

The only passengers are a large Barnsley family who are eating a bag of prawns without closing their mouths, or throwing any bits away. And the Britlings Chapel folk, who are singing over the thumping of the engines.

'Master the tempest is raging
The billows are tossing high.
The sky is overshadowed with blackness
No shelter or help is nigh.'

And the sea is absolutely calm at thirty-five minutes to low tide.

7

Not Much to Write
Home About

*Moustaches of yesterday, including the late King's –
And Miss Tidmarsh writes to Pa, twice.*

'Did.'

'Didn't.'

'They all had them and they all came right down their lips and they were all prickly,' Edna says.

'Weren't.'

Listen, at twenty-two minutes past ten, to Ada, Edna and Bess from Washing, side-by-side on a bench in a nook on South Side's shady Zig-Zag. They do not need the shade of course, for there is nothing but shade in Scarborough this July morning. They do need to sit. And Edna does need to be in the middle. Just listen to her.

'Men used goose grease to curl them up, Ada.'

'Didn't.'

'Did. You're just trying to aggravate me.'

'Not. And we're suffragettes and that means we think men are all shit-sharks today.'

'Yes, but they did used to wear lovely smells on them. Leather and flowers and that.'

'Didn't.'

'You never saw a man without a nice moustache them days. Now it's just drippy bits of bum fluff. And some don't even bother with that.'

'Do.'

But it is hard, even when you are a suffragette, not to look closely at the moustaches of the Zig-Zagging men who keep passing and touching their hats at you.

Edna says, 'Mind you, I like a beard as well. But you don't get them so much now with the younger ones. Only when they've got no chins.'

'Have.'

They stare waiting for a beard to Zig-Zag past.

Edna says, 'Most men with beards don't have much whiskers nowhere else. Old King Edward were bald all over bless him.'

Ada tugs Edna's hair. 'You'll be bald all over if you don't stop and all.'

An elderly man with a thick white moustache Zig-Zags past and raises his hat to Edna. Who twinkles.

But when he is gone she says, 'He weren't much to write home about.' And adds, 'Here, that reminds me.'

* * * * *

Mr Shephard and Miss Tidmarsh do not need reminding.

They are writing home from the fancy new Tudor post office on Aberdeen Walk in the very middle of town. Cards posted here before ten-thirty a.m. will be delivered this evening. It is a most useful facility for the conscientious day excursionist. If you write to yourself this morning, your card will be waiting for you tonight when you get home, to tell you where you've been.

And there is a crush of excursionists now, ten minutes before the last post, being conscientious and keeping warm.

Miss Tidmarsh writes her card at a sloping desk just like the one at work. She finishes it and turns it over to look at the copyright, tinted, real photograph of the Japanese Bridge in Peasholm Park she has never seen.

She turns the card over to read her message:

My dear Pa, Arrived here safely! Weather v. bracing. Hope you are feeling better! Your loving daughter Gwen xxxxx

'I wish he was dead, Trevor.'

'Sssh.'

'We shall die before them, of course.' The crowds press Miss Tidmarsh into her sloping desk. She turns and rips her postcard twice, and drops in on to the floor.

He says, 'This weather is so oppressive.'

'It's v. bracing.'

'And all this crush – '

'Why can't I enjoy myself on the one day when we're allowed to? My hat's ruined, my stocking is torn, I can't see properly through my spectacles. And now I'm going to be giddy.' She turns back to the desk she was writing at for something to hold. But there is a fat baby sitting on it now, being breast-fed by a bony woman from the brewery who smiles and says, 'Never stop, do they, bless them?'

Miss Tidmarsh shakes her head, breathes in and holds her breath.

'Here we are, Miss Tidmarsh.'

'What, Trevor?'

'A "copyright photograph of a splendid high tide on the new Marine Drive" is what it says here. Just look at that wave! It must be twice the height of the gas lamp.'

'It's for your mother.'

'I've posted hers. Come to my desk.'

'Who is it for, then?'

'I thought for the mantelpiece in my room. But I can always purchase another.' He licks and sticks a green halfpenny stamp on it. 'If you could just write a brief note on it now, or you will miss the post?'

So she writes, while he looks the other way:

Have met a young man! Am going to stay here with him
to try to make babies. It will be v. bracing. Will get v.v.
giddy. v.v.v. glad you are not here to spoil it. No love.
G.

And she writes Pa's name and her life's address, and passes the card to Mr Shephard.

'All done and dusted then, Miss Tidmarsh?'

'Would you like to read it?'

'I don't really think – besides. You'll miss the post.'

And he slides it into the posting box.

She shivers, giddy as a seagull. No wonder! Pa will certainly get his card with all the news now, just as she promised! And what news! What a pickle!

Except he won't, of course. For he never collects his own letters from behind the soft green curtain at the stained-glass front door of home, where everything smells of dust and sticky tonics. Collecting the letters to take in with his breakfast each morning is one of Gwendolyne's little jobs. So there is no need for her to shiver now – as long as she is back by breakfast.

'What next, Miss Tidmarsh?'

'Can't you call me Gwen?'

'Of course I, er. It's just that we do seem to be in constant danger of coming across workpeople everywhere.'

And they do. For at the door they meet Edna, Bess and Ada from Washing, arriving just in time to miss the ten-thirty post.

Edna says Mr Shephard seems to have caught a bit of sun.

Ada pulls Edna's hair.

And Mr Shephard touches his hat and says the weather does seem to be picking up.

And it does. Miss Tidmarsh and Mr Shephard can feel a warmth now as they step into Aberdeen Walk, pretending that they are not together, and a clock bangs out the half hour.

8

The Tide Turns

Mr Holles takes the plunge – Up on the Esplanade for half an hour – Jesus's helpful advice to the fishermen – More letters home and what they mean – The sun comes out just in time – The smell of roses – The ha'penny drops – Monkey and the monkey – The sea ceaseth.

Now then.

It's coming up to eleven o'clock And if you love flesh you have come to the right place at the right time.

Listen! It's Mr Holles!

'Time to strip for gym!' Mr Holles shouts as he backs, fully-clothed in his astonishing beano suit and boater, up the steps of Mr Rawlings's bathing van in North Bay. 'Lucky Jim!' he adds, going in and slamming the door.

The sea has almost dropped over the edge, but that won't stop Mr Holles's annual dip any more than it will stop the coming sunshine.

The fifty-three Britlings employees who love flesh, or their jobs, who have gathered here with Mr Wagstaff, poor Mrs Holles and the Girl, smile and wait.

Mr Holles is important enough, of course, for Mr Rawlings himself to be holding the horse. So it is Mr Rawlings who now calls, 'If there are any gentlemen employees who are desirous of a bracing dip, Rawlings has several vans immediately available for you.'

A gentleman employee calls, 'Go on, Waggy. Get that daft mackintosh off and give yourself a wash.'

Mr Rawlings adds, 'For the small price of four pence per gentleman you will have exclusive use of Rawlings's bathing drawers, the total privacy of Rawlings's bathing van and full use of towel. Ladies' facilities are provided at the Scalby end of the sands here at sunny Scarborough. Members of the Royal Family are among my clients, and they firmly recommend Rawlings's brine bathing to their subjects.'

The same gentleman employee calls, 'You get in that water, Waggy. Then Mr Holles can tiddle on you proper.'

The audience laughs. And hears music from inside the bathing van.

Mr Holles is singing. First he is a jockey. Then a magician. And now a mahogany baritone. What a card! He is singing a music-hall song about a swimming teacher who instructs young women. And a very good swimming teacher he must be too, for all his pupils learn to swim. Except the married women. The married women of course can't keep their mouths shut long enough! And drown themselves!

The unmusical, unmarried Mr Wagstaff leads the gentlemen employees' applause for the baritone's sentiments. Their wives smile.

Mr Holles calls from inside the van. 'I am now fully attired in your bathing drawers, Mr Rawlings. I shall make one final check of my sparging tool. Yes, it all seems to be working. Lovely.'

'Off we go then, Mr Holles.' Mr Rawlings clips the horse. The van rolls six inches towards the sea.

'A moment, Mr Rawlings!'

'Come come, Mr Holles. Set an example, sir.'

But Mr Rawlings clips the horse twice. The bathing van halts.

Mr Holles opens the door. And steps out, still in his holiday boater but wearing heavy woolly swimming drawers, with straps, and 'Rawlings' stretched across his stomach, in case he tries to go home in them.

He does not speak.

His head is bright red now you can see the shocking white of his body. It seems to be too small, like snowmen's always are.

He puts his finger on his lip. And even the seagulls settle quietly to watch.

First he does several dainty ballet twirls. His audience

peers up at him and wonders if he is already drunk. Last year it was at least mid-afternoon before he was encouraging those lads from Clogging to set fire to the basket chairs on Rhyl front. (But they do say, don't they, that once you really devote yourself to drinking it gets easier?)

Mr Holles rubs handfuls of Scarborough air into his blue-veined legs. He slaps Scarborough air on his shoulders, and drips it into his drawers. He bends and rubs it into his red cheeks. He cups a handful and gargles it.

He wriggles his toes in the air, closes his eyes and, with his arms rigid as if he is sleep-walking, he sleep-walks down the steps.

And only now does his audience realize the silent joke!

For he is pretending to be someone from the pictures, of course. One of those funny bad men who are always fat and always have twinkling eyes and thick naughty moustaches. And Mr Holles is pretending to be one of those going for a dip in the pretend North Sea.

He clears his nose, one nostril at a time. He gargles air and spits it. He sinks into the pretend sea – ankles, blue legs, tummy, shoulders and chin.

And isn't it cold! You can feel that pretend water gurgling into your own holes and crannies. You can feel that rusty anchor (or is it a shark?) ripping into you, too, and dragging you down to the skeletons of sailors who have been swaying down there since Noah pretended to come to Scarborough to have a go on the steamer, just before the Flood. (Just like you.)

And now you hold your breath until Mr Holles struggles free and then shoots up through the water to the air, spluttering and spitting, a second before he would have to pretend to suffocate for ever.

You have to applaud. Mr Holles pulls his moustaches, and peers round a pretend rock to see if he is safe for his next piece of villainy.

But what will it be?

He turns away. He pretends to whistle as he raises his boater to pretend people he pretends to be passing. But look now! He's suddenly weeing in the pretend sea. You can feel the pretend sea getting warmer.

And now – it always happens, doesn't it, just when you've started and when you can't stop – someone sees him. And it's poor Mrs Holles! Mr Holles covers his eyes. Look how ashamed he is, trying to cover his marriage tackle, trankle-ments and trolley-bobs by squirming his thighs together as he wades chest high away from Mrs Holles. But look now, his drawers are hooked by the shark, or the anchor, or whatever it is that isn't there that is sharp. And he tears his clothes and covers himself with his fat hand while he plunges up for safety to the steps of Mr Rawlings's bathing van.

The door slams shut on him. What a card! Mr Wagstaff begins the applause.

Mr Rawlings clips the horse again. And Mr Holles is driven out to sea.

His employees run after the bathing van down to the real North Sea to watch the repeat performance. Or at least to be seen there by him as he drowns, so they are kept on at the brewery by his executors.

Only poor Mrs Holles and the maid and Mr Wagstaff stay, looking out to sea.

What a card though! The galloping horse at the station! The newspaper that flew at York! That portable what-not for Mr Wagstaff! And now he's in the pictures!

Mr Wagstaff raises his hat to Mrs Holles. 'I must apologize on behalf of the employees for their disappointing turn-out. I am sure you will agree that there has been in no way any failure of organization or of information.'

Mrs Holles nods. And Mr Wagstaff winks at her again.

Blessed are not the meek. Mr Holles inherits all of us.

'Mr Wagstaff,' poor Mrs Holles says, clutching his mackin-toshed sleeve. 'Where is the wooden pier?'

And she explains about the last family holiday, and her father, and how Mr Holles is now stealing her memory so that she cannot even be happy thinking of the past. Father's waistcoat smelt of soap. And she had cut her knee at the end of the wooden pier, and that was why he was carrying her. And to get on to that wooden pier she had run up a grassy hill to the flagpoles that got taller. And the pier was suddenly there, like a great bridge driving straight out to sea. Here, at Scarborough.

Mr Wagstaff sneezes. He says he wishes he could be more

helpful. Indeed, if there were such a pier as she is describing at Scarborough it would be fully detailed in his Illustrative Programme. And it is not.

He apologizes that he must leave her now in this distressed condition, but he does have a full day's programme of duties in connection with the excesses of the employees. And Mr Holles will soon be returning from his famous dip to look after her. But meanwhile she has the maid.

And Mr Wagstaff goes.

He will take the tram from Peasholm up Columbus Ravine and back into town. He will leave a note for Mr Holles at the Grand Hotel and walk down the Zig-Zag on to the front. There he will turn up his mackintosh collar and enter the foyer of the Palladium Picture House where he will purchase a 1/6d ticket. He will go into the dark halfway through a continuous showing of *The Sacrifice of Kathleen*.

* * * * *

And it is morning parade time upon the Esplanade.

If the sun is parading this morning it will have to hurry. Every important person in Scarborough is already out.

Raise your hats and murmur and smile, safely above the trippers and the fisherfolk and the sea.

Cocky Mr Atkinson, his aunts and the blonde have only come to watch from a bench high above the Spa.

But there is plenty to watch. You can enjoy, from now until lunchtime, the finest East Coast parade of men and women and nannies and chaperons and chaperons' chaperons. Strolling up and down as if they owned the whole of Yorkshire, which between them they probably do. Listen to them exchanging views on the weather, and admiring the graceful curving hotels, and arranging marriages and adultery, from now until lunch. (For we are all the same aren't we, under the many layers of fine clothes and good manners? There is just as much heartburn here as there will be this afternoon in the courting hour when the trippers unbutton, far below the Esplanade people.)

See and be seen here if you are anyone, or ever want to be, in a cloud of scent and cigars and roses.

But do hurry, for you can never tell how long the summer is going to last.

After half an hour of watching, Mr Atkinson suggests to the blonde that they go to the open-air pictures. The aunts overhear and agree that it would be most educational. They have never seen it. Mr Atkinson looks less cocky.

And as they all stroll down the sloping path from the Esplanade to the Cliff Bridge and then by lift go to the Fore-shore Road and the Palladium Picture House, the sun gets ready to come out.

* * * * *

You can feel the sun even in the narrow red slums in the old town behind the harbour.

Owen in red tie and sandals notices through the tiny win-dow of the small back room where four comrades discuss what is to be done.

He presents fraternal greetings from home, as they begin writing the new pamphlet. And he kicks off his sandals under the table.

* * * * *

The rock-pools in South Bay are beginning to dazzle in the brightening morning.

Tommy, Spud and Monkey are barefoot, fishing crabs with a holey shrimp net. Their boots are lined up like Tommy says they are in the Baptist Boys Club.

Monkey drinks sea-water to make him taller like Spud says it does.

'Jesus were a fisherman,' Tommy says.

'Jesus is dead,' says Spud.

'Not.'

They scoop a hank of seaweed at Monkey.

'You can taste the fish in the water, can't you, Tommy?' says Monkey.

Spud says, 'Anyroad, I thought Jesus were reckoned to be a carpenter last I heard about him.'

They fish some more, catching nothing. Then Tommy says, 'All his pals went fishing. And when they weren't catching nowt he told 'em to put their net down on the other side and have a miracle.'

'Lend it us,' Spud says, taking the net and putting it behind him to fish. 'Nowt.'

'That's cos you don't believe.' Tommy takes the net back

and fishes. 'Jesus won't do things if you ask him.'

Spud grabs the net back, snaps the cane and throws it at Monkey. 'I'm going to kill you, mental.'

Tommy says, 'You go off and do some begging, Monkey. Then we'll buy ourselves some fish over there.'

'Yeah, Tommy, thanks. And Tommy, I believe in miracles, Tommy.'

'Mental,' Spud says.

* * * * *

And Ada, Edna and Bess from Washing are still in the new post office. They stand side-by-side at the sloping desks with Edna safely in the middle.

Edna is showing them what she knows about stamps. 'It's a secret language for courting with.'

'Isn't.'

'It is, Ada, in case your boyfriend's mother finds out. What you do is put your postage stamp in a different place, and it doesn't matter what you write when she reads it. Like if you put it up here – ' and she places her unlicked stamp sideways in the top left-hand corner above THIS SPACE MAY BE USED FOR COMMUNICATION ' – that means "I hate you".'

'Waste of a stamp if you hate him,' Ada says. 'And what does this mean?' She slides the card into the posting box without the stamp, which flutters on to the floor.

'What did you do that for?'

'We're not wasting good stamps on menfolk.'

'He'll have to pay now.'

'Good. That's what us suffragettes believe, right, Bess?'

'Mmm.'

'Who *you* been writing to, Bess?'

'Myself.' And she has.

'Have a stamp, then,' Ada says, licking Edna's and placing it top left, upside down, on Bess's card, and posting it. 'And we'll have a kitty from now on.'

* * * * *

The sky outside the post office is as blue now as a twopenny ha'penny postage stamp, with its solemn picture of the last king of England who'll ever have a beard.

And, with a click like the electric lights, all the colours are switched on and it is summer.

86

The sun rolls in from Flamborough, soars over South Cliff golf links and parades down the Esplanade, on to the Cliff Bridge, along the Foreshore Road, and past the Tepid Sea Bathing.

It blinds the last of the Scotch fishergirls at the harbour, and the herring boats that have missed the tide, and the sleeping white lighthouse.

It dashes round the corner on to Marine Drive without paying the toll and climbs all the seagulled slopes above it, right up to the castle.

Everything is warm and bright. Everything smells more.

And everything is possible again at Scarborough in July, now that the sun is having the morning off as well.

* * * * *

And the ancient blacksmith smells the sun as he sits alone on a bench in the Rosary on South Cliff. He is poking at his pipe with a twig of sharpened hedge as he smells the morning. And all the blowing roses smell like roses used to do when he was a child.

He says, 'Bugger.'

* * * * *

Higher up on the next hill towards Whitby, Spaldy is biting his unlit pipe. He has still not begun his painting, even though the sun is shining full tilt up here now. So it is not the sun he has been waiting for, twenty minutes before low tide?

He rubs his eyes with the corner of his hanky and, now, when at last no one is around, he leaves his paints and slips a ha'penny into the telescope slot to look.

* * * * *

There's so much to paint Spaldy – look!

And so little time left now.

Why aren't you painting? What's wrong? What do you see that dries up your painting?

That widow from the pub next to the cemetery in a hat made from today's *Times* newspaper, chasing a seagull with a bun?

Those sad, hollow-backed donkeys who trudge the sunny beaches all summer and never see beyond the harbour?

The escapologist who escapes twenty times every day and is back there every morning?

Those giggling, hobble-skirted Gibson girls, sequined with sand from where they have fallen in their sack races into the crowd of weeping children watching Punch murder babies?

That man from the brewery at the top of the helter-skelter, releasing his pigeon from his snotty hanky and finding its wings have snapped?

Or will you paint that professor in chains, riding his motor cycle into the oily harbour while his wife counts farthings in their Capstan tobacco tin?

That clogger from the brewery, strapped into the chair by the pier, having his last three teeth pulled out for nothing by that professor of teeth, who has charged the sandy crowd a ha'penny each, and promised blood?

Will you paint the blood, Spaldy, as this summer mid-morning clots and the sea goes still?

Paint the sea itself then, for the sea is as surprised as everybody else by how far it has dared to go out this morning.

The ha'penny drops. Spaldy steps back, bangs his nose on the brass eyepiece, and bleeds.

* * * * *

Monkey bleeds, too, in the small menagerie on South Sands where they are tormenting the animals instead of buying fish. There are only six cages, and only doves and a painted rabbit. And a monkey.

Spud says the monkey must be mental.

Monkey asks the mester if he can hold him.

Tommy says, ' "The sea ceaseth and it sufficeth us." Done it!'

'Eh?'

'It's a holy tongue-twister, Spud. If you say it right, it shows Jesus loves you.'

* * * * *

And it's nine minutes past eleven now in the sunshine of Scarborough.

And still more than seven hours of beano left.

Miss Tidmarsh and Mr Shephard are walking on the edge of the sea far out in front of the Spa, with coats, gloves, guidebooks and best black shoes.

There are no waves. The sea has stopped.

Miss Tidmarsh and Mr Shephard stand separate, facing Europe. She holds a long shaving strop of seaweed.

'You can tell the future from seaweed,' he says.

'Can you?'

'Well, I cannot of course. I'm afraid there are so many things I cannot do.'

' "There are many things you can do at the seaside that you cannot do at home" . . . It was a song I heard the Electric Light party singing at York.'

'Ah, a song.'

They walk on.

He says, 'Seaweed is probably a natural barometer. Do you think that could be it? Like pine cones?'

'When Mother was alive we went to the Peak District and I was allowed to bring back a pine cone, so that I could forecast the weather for my diary. When it closed there was going to be rain. And when it opened there was sunshine. Or vice versa. I would not be much help in forecasting if I cannot even remember – I'm talking too much, Trevor.'

'I like you to talk. In fact – '

But he has to skip round a small pink jellyfish, and they walk on silently on the dying edge of the North Sea for some time. Then he adds, 'I do believe the Welsh people eat seaweed.'

'Do they?'

'I must look it up in Mummy's *Pears* when I get back.'

They walk on separately. They do not pace out a message in the wet sand in their best black shoes – 'Miss Tidmarsh loves Mr Shephard. Mr Shephard loves Miss Tidmarsh.' Yet no workpeople would see it here written in sand for one moment at lowest tide. Miss Tidmarsh and Mr Shephard are as silent now about their love as are the gulls and fish and skeletons and sandworms, wind and sun.

For Tommy was right.

The sea ceaseth!

Miss Tidmarsh and Mr Shephard are dusty people who whisper invoices and live in dusty curtained rooms with locked pianos, mints and tonic medicines. But even they now almost hear the turning of the tide this strangest of mornings.

For, exactly on time, as foretold in the Illustrative Programme and the guidebooks and Mr Holles's lost newspaper and the tide tables at the harbour forecasting a certain future for ever – the sea changes its mind!

It is an extraordinary moment that happens twice every day for ever.

If Miss Tidmarsh or Mr Shephard had ever watched the beer brewed at the brewery they invoice, their metaphor for this extraordinariness might be the moment the fermentation starts and the bubbles come. If they had met earlier in their lives perhaps the fluttering of wombs? If they were Spaldy, the first splash of paint on the canvas?

But what metaphors for Miss Tidmarsh and Mr Shephard, whose world has never been suddenly new again? Their own love, never spoken, that could make their world new, but isn't doing, halfway through the beano?

And it is too late for metaphors anyway.

For with a flick of a seagull's claw the silence has gone.

And the tide has turned. And pours now on to four best black shoes.

Mr Shephard squeaks and dances sideways. He falls towards Miss Tidmarsh and she almost tumbles herself, as she avoids being touched.

She throws the seaweed at the first tiny waves.

'I rather thought you wished to take that home to add to your collection?'

'No,' she says. And then, 'What I do wish is that we could enjoy ourselves. But I keep thinking it's nearly over.'

They shake their shoes and stand back a little.

The wind has changed with the tide.

'I can hear music!' Miss Tidmarsh frowns.

'I believe I can also,' Mr Shephard says.

They listen.

'It is Wagner's *Die Meistersinger*!' Miss Tidmarsh cries. 'From the morning concert on the Spa. With Mr Maclean's orchestra.'

'Ah.'

'I thought I was imagining!' she giggles.

They listen, to make sure they are not imagining.

The wind shifts and they now hear seagulls and the weekly children sandcastling at Children's Corner.

Miss Tidmarsh says, 'I was reading about Richard Wagner for when we came here. In case we decided to spend our morning on the Spa. He fell in love with the wife of the conductor Hans von Bülow and she bore him three children. And yet he was fifty-seven years old before they could break free and marry each other.'

'Ah.'

'Isn't that remarkable? Waiting until you are fifty-seven before you dare to be happy?'

Mr Shephard nods. They stare at the waxing North Sea and listen to the waves, gulls and shouts until just before noon, when the sun goes in.

* * * * *

But never mind the sun. What about the lovers? Shall we sneak a look at tonight's fuzzy beano photograph to see if they are any happier by the time it's all over? Cheat and look at the end, as if the beano is only a novel? Will they have enjoyed anything, will they have touched, by home-time? Will he have popped his question? Will she have said she will?

Yes, look at the photograph . . . You will not see them there straight away. But look more carefully. Miss Tidmarsh and Mr Shephard are hidden people, and a nervous photographer might easily miss them first time.

But they aren't on his picture, are they, however hard you look?

PART FOUR

9

Snap

*Cooks and mermaids and pierrots and survivors – The hope of
the world – The seagulls' strategies for lunch – News of the
blacksmith's blocked pipe – Miss Tidmarsh and Mr Shephard
stroll on the South Side with the guidebooks – How to fiddle
the trams and the advantage of ragged trousers – A warning
for Mr Wilcock – The future partly revealed for half-a-crown –
Lunch and a song at the Grand.*

It's about time for lunch now.

But who's made the lunches, all boiled and steamed and
baked and browned and grilled, in every kitchen from Mr
Truefitt's Astoria Hotel high on South Cliff, to the Corpora-
tion's Rocks at Scalby Mills?

It might be holidays for some. But what about the maids
and waitresses and barmen and cooks and clerks? What
about the workers, eh?

And what about the three mermaids at the Underground
Palace now balancing on their tails in front of two disappointed young men and a fisherman?

And what about the seven Catlin pierrots on South Sands,
performing their French song and juggling onions? And
George Royle's Merry Imps on the North Side, seven men
and four women, the first mixed pierrot troupe in the world,
singing in sailor suits about a sausage made out of grey
stockings?

They are all working. Fun to you, work to them.

And what of the staring man with the tin, outside the
Seamen's Bethel by the harbour? Working to raise a fund for
Titanic survivors like himself? And he will be working again

this afternoon too (and doing slightly better business) when he will be a chattering survivor of Captain Scott's last journey to the South Pole, outside the main railway station. What an unfortunate double victim of history this worker is – and history might not have finished with him yet, of course.

Yes, what about the workers this Scarborough lunchtime?

* * * * *

'To the workers of the world. The hope of the world,' Owen, in red tie, calls as he crumbles his cheese at the table in the slum house where he has been working all sunshine. Another comrade has come now from Harrogate to join them, and their morning's work is completed with the first draft of the new leaflet.

It calls on the workers to stop what's coming.

The comrade from Manchester next to Owen grunts, 'Not much hope of them coming to a meeting, mind you.'

'You came,' Owen says.

'Aye – five on us from all Yorks. and Lancs.'

Owen grins. 'It looked more convenient on the map when I planned it.'

'We'll remember that in Lancashire, when the time comes and map-reading might be a bit of use.'

'The bosses make the lying maps, see.'

'Nay Owen, they don't make owt. That's like saying Pharaohs built the pyramids, and they never touched a brick in all their lives. Workers made everything. A bit wobbly, your socialism and geography, this side of the Pennines. If you ask me.'

Owen seems to smell warm oatcakes. He says, 'Aye, well. We'll sort that out after the revolution, brother.'

'I wouldn't mind a few more here now helping to sort it out.'

'We'll have to start without them and they can join us when they wake up,' Owen says.

'You're sure they will?'

'It's as sure as . . . this morning.' With the smell of oatcakes and the candle.

The Manchester comrade grunts, 'You want to get a boat to Paris. That's where the workers' history is being made while we sit at the seaside.'

Owen looks.

And the woman comrade from Harrogate, who has to get home before her husband does, picks up the draft. She says, 'We'll have to get on, comrades. There's not long.'

* * * * *

The seagulls are in no particular rush, though it is time they were off for their lunches, too. There is food to be beaked everywhere.

Mind you, Scarborough's a good place to be a seagull. All the rival armies who have come to feed the worms, and all the gardens, and the delicate rich people who have come to see them and who cannot finish their rich meals here! And long before them there were fishermen who came to churn up the seas. And then the Spa water bubbled. And then came the railway, of course, with thousands of lunches arriving on it every hour in the summer.

No seagull worth his sea-salt stays perched and squawking on the crumbling cliff above the harbour in the summer. And there are so many of them with all the good food. The hill is beginning to crumble under their weight. (And what will the seagulls do then, poor things?)

But this July lunchtime is not the time for such worries. We might none of us be here this time next year . . .

Go pecking down to the two beaches and the trippers who throw lardy cake and orange peel at you. Or wait an hour for your lunch to be scraped off the starched tablecloths and china plates into the stinking back yards of the 10/6d hotels.

Or float out to the fishing smacks and cobles and steamers, scattering your lunch all along the coast.

Or claw inland as far as Malton, where the worms are notorious, or Great Driffield, where there is a great rubbish heap.

* * * * *

The ancient blacksmith with the blocked pipe is lunching in a fried fish café near the Picturedrome on Westborough. When the waitress isn't looking, he pokes his blocked pipe with his bent fish fork.

The beano's about half over, and he's not had a draw on his pipe all day.

Bugger, isn't it?

Meanwhile Miss Tidmarsh and Mr Shephard are standing at the open gate of the South Cliff tramway to the cliff top. They are the only passengers, and the lift is waiting there with the faint sounds of Gounod's ballet music from *Faust* now leaking from the Spa bandstand so that they can hear it free. They stand facing seawards, waiting for the view that the guidebook recommends from the lift.

Miss Tidmarsh tells Mr Shephard how Gounod was accused of stealing a whole opera from a younger musician, who later died insane. And how somehow that mirrors the whole Faust legend, doesn't it, with the selling of your soul for just a short moment of success?

She adds, 'I'm so sorry, Trevor. I'm afraid I do rather prattle when I get the chance. Pa always says.'

'Not at all. I'm just sorry I'm not musical like you.'

'I did once think I might become a concert pianist. But Pa forbade the piano when mother was first ill and it has never since been unlocked.'

Mr Shephard opens his mouth. 'Gw—'

But a large family of permanent visitors bark and laugh and bustle into the lift. Miss Tidmarsh and Mr Shephard go up the car to the far end, and sit on the long slatted seat. So when the tram jerks up its three hundred feet by brine-water power they miss the recommended view and the sudden shocking moment when you realize how much sea there is . . .

They walk on up the Esplanade admiring the sweeping hotels the guidebooks draw their attention to. They turn left into the discreet Italian Gardens, down the symmetrical steps to the stone-curbed lily pond with its fat fish under the grey-blue statue in a hat and not much else, standing on one leg. All the seats recommended by the guidebooks here are busy with visitors who know each other. They raise hats and murmur as they stroll past the less smartly turned out brewery clerks who have been travelling in their clothes since last night.

Miss Tidmarsh says, 'The statue, I believe, is Mercury, Trevor. He stole oxes from Apollo on the day he was born. And he invented the lyre – l-y-r-e. And he was not only the god of thieves. And of elephants.' She giggles. 'He is also the god of shepherds.'

'Of shepherds?' Mr Shephard nods. 'Really?' And he looks up from the guidebook. For help.

They climb up the southward steps of the Italian Gardens, as the guidebook suggests, and up to the sombre Shuttleworth clock placed right at the end of South Cliff to warn you, with its four little faces, that it is twenty past twelve on beano day and four-ninths of your holiday have gone. Or so Miss Tidmarsh optimistically calculates.

Though she does not say.

Five children in sailor suits who care nothing for passing time (yet) play kiss-catch in the arches of Mr Shuttleworth's clock. How easy it is to kiss when you are young, Miss Tidmarsh thinks.

But she does not say that, either.

Mr Shephard checks his watch against Mr Shuttleworth's four clocks. 'Taking into account the map, I suggest that we do just have time to stroll down through Holbeck Gardens and then back along the seafront, to the Spa itself, entering there by the entrance just beyond the tramway. It will then be more or less one o'clock, which is the hour the Spa afternoon session begins, and we can get complete value for our ninepence.'

They stroll down the steep path of Holbeck Gardens, heading out now beyond Scarborough towards the raw cliffs of the North Sea. They look at the wild flowers there, and cannot name them. And they separate for each party of gasping weekly visitors who come laughing up with diabolos and hampers and rugs and vacuum flasks for their lunches.

'Ah?' For now, where several steep paths swoop down and cross, there is a stone hut structure, not mentioned in the guidebook, with a tap in the middle. Miss Tidmarsh wonders if the water would be safe to drink. Mr Shephard thinks it probably is. The guidebooks in fact generally praise the water of Scarborough – both the spa waters he and Miss Tidmarsh hope to indulge in a little later, and the domestic supplies.

They cross to the tap and discover an old tin saucer of water on the ground. Miss Tidmarsh remembers home where Pa sits in front of the bubbling gas fire with a saucer of water in front.

There is a metal plate with a message. Mr Shephard reads it

solemnly. ' "In Loving Memory of Hubert Alderson Smith, Lieutenant 1st Battalion East Yorkshire Regiment, eldest son of George Alderson Smith of White Croft Cliff, Scarborough JPDL, who died at Cairo Oct 17 1895. A monument erected by his brother officers marks his last resting place in the cemetery at Cairo." '

Miss Tidmarsh changes her mind and does not drink. They walk on down the switchback paths through the hills of meadowsweet and brown butterflies, and the sea suddenly appears again, vast, and noisy, above rocks.

Miss Tidmarsh looks along the semi-circle coast of South Bay, and thinks it is all too much for one day's beano. They should not have come.

Mr Shephard calls, 'Oh, I did notice, by the way, in the guidebook, that there is a photographer on the Spa itself. Provided they do not take too lengthy a lunch we should be able to obtain a sitting for you before the afternoon concert, for your portrait?' He nods. 'And if I may – I would like to pay for it as a small present and a token of what I – '

'I want *you* on it!' she shouts, and her voice sounds to her just like Pa's always does when he calls her from the other end of the dusty house to move his pillow or turn the gas down a little.

* * * * *

Five-and-twenty past twelve.

Tommy, Monkey and Spud are lunching off a shared stick of humbug rock on the harbour wall, and discussing the best way to fiddle the trams.

Spud says, 'When conductor comes round, I ask for the wrong place. He says, "You're on the wrong tram, sonny" so I get off next stop. And then get on the one behind.'

Tommy shakes his head. 'Tell them you're going on to hymn practice and you thought the tram were going the other way. And then flit.'

Monkey says, 'I feel in me pocket and cry and tell them me money's fell out.'

'Mental,' Spud says.

'I do. Look.' He tugs the pocket from his trousers, and shows them the ragged hole.

'That's so you can play with your thing,' Tommy says.

'Isn't, Tommy.'

'You're always playing with it, and Jesus says you're not to.'

'I'm not, Tommy. Not always.' And then, 'Anyroad, it's mine.'

Spud says, 'He's mental. It won't make no odds.'

Tommy says, 'Jesus sees you through walls.'

Monkey slips his pocket back in his trousers. And keeps his hand in.

* * * * *

Five-and-twenty to one, and the sun comes out again for six minutes.

But the suffragettes from Washing miss it because they are upstairs in the milky steam of Mr Wilcock's Dining Rooms on the front just before the Rock Shop and the Arcadia.

'And the café windows run with steam so that even from the window seat Bess cannot see the waves.

'Not my fault,' Edna says. 'And you'd not be laughing if your water gave you trouble.'

'I'm not laughing. And you wouldn't have trouble with your water if you didn't sup so much tea.'

'And it's because of me water I do sup, Bess love.' And she pours another brown cupful. 'And anyroad it's Ada we're waiting for.'

'Only cos we've had to wait that long for you dashing in and out of that lav, making eyes at Mr Wilcock.'

'That's only a bit of daft, love.'

'We reckon to be suffragettes.'

'It's votes for women we want, Bess. We're not against tantalizing men.'

'I've noticed.'

'You've let yourself get bitter. Whoops. I've gone blind. No, it's someone with their big warm hands over my eyes, hope he's nice.'

It is. But he's not. It's Mr Wilcock. 'Is everything quite all right, ladies?'

'No,' Bess says.

'Oh dear, dear. Now I wonder what we can do about that?' Mr Wilcock purrs.

'You can stop doing that,' Edna giggles, 'unless you know what you're starting.'

And Bess says to the cruet, 'Tell him to get his windows cleaned so we can see the sea we've come all this way to see. Tell him it might help if there was a few women's lavatories in Scarborough. We've noticed that men don't have to queue up indoors in stinking cafés all day, buying pots of tea.'

Mr Wilcock says, 'Oh deary, deary me.'

Edna begins to say something.

Ada comes across.

And Bess stares at Wilcock. 'We're suffragettes. You wait while we've got the vote. We'll have things different then.'

Edna says, 'You're not allowed, Bess. He's a man. Aren't you Mr Wilcock – ow, Ada!'

Bess stares at Ada.

Ada says, 'Shush love, it'll be all right in a bit.'

* * * * *

But will it?

It's not been all right so far for Madame, the palmist, clairvoyante and crystal reader in her tiny booth off Sandside. It's been a very poor morning indeed. Who could have guessed that the sun would have come out again, slap in the middle of Friday, just when folk are getting scared about the rest of their lives, and start dropping in to ask if it's true they've got to go home?

So Madame has one arm in her coat and is about to go off for a lunchtime drink, when the first customer, in a pink headscarf, pokes round the Persian drapery.

'You open, Madame?'

'The future is always open to genuine seekers, my dear.'

'That's us.' Lizzie tugs Percy inside.

He scowls. 'Will you give over pushing and pulling me? This collar's murder.'

'I'm paying, so shush.'

Madame lets her coat drop on the floor, and takes a cloudy glass egg from her drawer. 'Close the curtain on the material world outside, my dear,' she incants. 'You've come at a crossroads in your lives together.'

'Told you it'd be good, Perce.' Lizzie tugs the curtains shut. 'What do we have to do, Madame?'

'First, silver passes from your palm to mine as a token of your seriousness. For half-a-crown I fortunately can offer an immediate consultation on health, finance and love, taking you from now till your happy quiet deaths in your own bed. For a further – '

'Bed!' Lizzie squeaks.

'Half-a-crown!' Percy says.

Madame says she can only help the genuine traveller, but they must not waste her time. She is already missing an important engagement. She has read palms for royalty, and senior members of the Yorkshire aristocracy. And, this season, for the pierrot troupes of both bays.

She turns to Lizzie, who is paying. 'You and your husband will not always be alone. Nor will – '

'Husband, Percy? You listen to this.'

'She must be right good.'

Madame smiles. Her teeth are very white. In the dark of her Persian booth she might even be a real gypsy. 'There are many kinds of marriage and many kinds of husbands. And some marriages never happen, though they should. And could, if we only knew what future we miss.'

'Sit down, Percy,' Lizzie orders. He does. 'We'll have the lot.' She puts half-a-crown on the table and sits on Percy's knee.

Madame shakes her head. 'Palm crystal cards. Health love finance. For half-a-crown?'

'Half-a-crown's all we've got.'

Madame shakes her head.

Lizzie says, 'Then we'll just have the love.'

Madame shakes her head, 'Palms cards *and* crystal? For half-a-crown, for both of you?'

Lizzie shakes her head. 'Just do one of them, it's the same future coming for us whatever you look at, isn't it? Just do us half-a-crown's worth. We're missing us beano.'

Madame shakes her head. And begins.

Lizzie will have one child. Her husband will go away for a while.

Lizzie drops her hat box. Cake confettis on to the Persian carpet.

Percy puts out his palm. Madame shakes her head.

'Where's Bunty?'

Madame shakes her head again.

Meanwhile, the ozone and the bracing dip have done a good morning's work for Mr Holles, so he has an even finer appetite this late lunchtime than usual.

He is not wasting it as he sits in the Grand Hotel dining-room between poor Mrs Holles and the Girl, on the long window table facing in at all the other diners.

He taps the young wine waiter's knuckles with his fish knife. 'We'll have another bottle of your Burgundy wine, lad. The York ham was too salty, and the first Mrs Holles here reckons her lamb chop was fusty, and she's eaten nothing but the watercress.'

'Sir.'

'Trouble is, her memory's going now, poor thing. You might not think so to look at us, lad, but she's several years younger than me.'

'Sir.'

'She came to Scarborough with her father once before. She remembers very clearly being carried down a wooden pier with him. Just beyond a bandstand and some flagpoles. She was telling my flunkey, Wagstaff, all about it.'

Poor Mrs Holles shudders and does not look up from the spoon she is clutching.

And Mr Holles continues, 'And of course Mr Wagstaff, my flunkey, told me in a full report he left me here at the Grand. But it turns out that there was no wooden pier that Mrs Holles remembers. Poor Mrs Holles who tells tales to servants and can't even remember properly when she was happy.'

'Sir.'

'Still, you just remember the Burgundy, lad, and you'll do fine.'

'Sir.' And he goes.

Mr Holles taps the Girl's plump fingers with the fish knife. 'I do like a girl with appetite. In fact –' He stands up. 'I'm going to sing a song about it. I shall be remembering all the words, and all the tune. Unlike some people who can remember nothing. Your attention please, fellow diners!'

He bangs his glass with his fish knife, and when he has their attention he says, 'My name is Holles. This is the first Mrs Holles and bursting out of her plump uniform here is my

104

beautiful assistant. Now there was once a man who took a girl out to dine. She had an amazing appetite but he did not have much money. As you will hear. It is a beautiful song, beautifully remembered.'

The song, sung in a light unexpected baritone, is much appreciated. And he does remember all the words.

Poor Mrs Holles watches the Girl, all plump dimples and teeth. She must be told about him as soon as there is a chance. Before her life is destroyed. Yes, Mr Holles is a man who can make any room laugh, and can dance and sing. But afterwards . . .

The song ends. Mr Holles calls for his nephew, Alan Atkinson, from the far corner where he has been sitting with his aunts and the blonde, and where he is now applauding with the rest of the room. Mr Holles introduces Alan to the dining-room and explains the present state of the brewing trade which, briefly, is that the breweries are only being kept open for the sake of the employees and the customers.

Mrs Holles looks at the two of them. Notices that Alan Atkinson already has the same hard family face and the same shiny skin, with no wrinkles round the eyes for all their laughing. It is of, course, the face that her own children will have. Unless –

'Whereas I'd say your blonde's got an appetite. Get her some oysters this afternoon. The Girl's going to have some.' And Mr Holles pours Burgundy for himself and the Girl. He spills some on the tablecloth. He says it is like blood on a sheet. He calls for puddings.

'Spotted dick for the girls, eh?'

In the Swim

*The stowaways get ready for their swim – Albert and Flossie
decide not to risk a late lunch of butterscotch – Advice if you're
going courting – Parasols and guns at the photographers – The
couple who want to halt time – And what Mr Holles and
Mr Wagstaff do next.*

Tommy, Spud and Monkey are undressing by the dark rocks
at Scalby in North Bay, where no one sits even on a July
afternoon.

Monkey says, 'You taking all yours off, Tommy?'

'Course he is, mental, he's not getting them wet.' Spud
stands on one leg, picking black bits from between his toes,
and sniffing them.

Tommy says, 'In the Holy Land where Jesus comes from
there's a sea that's all salt. And – ', he tugs at his squeaking
corduroy trousers but they won't undo, ' – you can't drown
in that even when you want to.'

'Who says?' Spud asks, swapping feet.

'The Primitive Methods.'

'Waggy's lot?'

'Yeah.'

'You're not in them.'

'Were when they did the Dead Sea.' He yanks at his
trousers.

'So you could go to Blackpool!'

'Didn't go to Blackpool.'

'You got barred for smashing that window.'

Tommy rips open his trousers. 'Them Chapel beanos are
tripe anyway. It's all women and kids.'

Monkey says, 'Didn't know your mam stitched you into your trousers like my mam does me, Tommy.'

'She don't!' Tommy yells. And then louder, 'And I did smash window. After Waggy chucked me out. Here, it's raining!'

And Tommy steps out of his trousers and pisses a crucifix into the sand. Spud aims at Monkey.

'Tell him, Tommy!'

'Oh soz, didn't see you,' Spud says, spraying Monkey's shirt instead.

And naked he tiptoes to the black and green rocks, looking in the dazzled ponds for things to eat.

Tommy yells, ' "The sea ceaseth and it sufficeth us!" ' at the sun, which slides behind another white cloud.

Naked, Monkey looks out at the North Sea. How do boats stay up? Is it like Tommy's salt, where Jesus lives?

The afternoon snoozes.

Tommy dangles a purple starfish and watches it shiver in the sunshine. He skims it along the sands towards Europe.

'Was it dead, Tommy?'

'It is now, poor sinner. It's a blessed release.'

Spud throws a dead crab at Monkey's bare bum.

When Monkey turns, Spud whoops, 'Here, look at Monkey's thing!'

'Yours does same too, don't it Tommy? On trams and that.'

Spud says, 'Has it got Scarborough writ right through it? Let's have a look, Monkey? Or I'll kill you.'

* * * * *

Just as Albert and Flossie peer through the window of the South Sands Refreshment Room near the underground People's Palace, thinking of late lunching.

'What they got, Albie?'

Albert reads, ' "Bread and cheese threepence. Plate of cold meat sixpence. Tea threepence. Butterscotch per packet sixpence." '

'Nay, butterscotch'd be a bit clarty after all us beer, me old.' Flossie's cap falls off, and he pats his head with his white silk scarf.

'Aye, well, you can pay them a penny,' Albert reads, 'for a borrow of plate, knife, fork, mustard and salt, if you bring your own provisions.'

'We haven't, have we?'

'No.'

'Stick to beer then. Don't want us stomachs upsetting.'

* * * * *

It is time for courting now whether your stomach is upset or not. I'd enjoy myself if I were you. It's a nice warm afternoon. Might do your lumbago good? Shake your liver up a bit more? Nobody knows you here. You probably don't even know the person you're courting. And nobody'll mind if you make a bit of a mess.

All the ticklings and the strokings and pokings and bitings and lickings and huggings and pressings that are possible now as the sun comes out and you hide from it with someone else's body!

Listen to all the giggling, too, for courting here is fun and safe, or nearly, with all of us together in the Scarborough afternoon.

'They're off.'

'Geeo'er.'

Giggle away, but it's serious too. It's all that will be talked about tomorrow. And it's what you'll remember every July for ever, with any smell of seaweed or the laugh of any seagull.

'Go on then if you're going to.'

'You keeping your hat on?'

This is what most of us young ones have been looking forward to. Ever since the beano was announced last October and Britlings started deducting threepence every week.

'How far do you want to go?'

'All way, don't you?'

'I mean into these bushes, daft.'

The guidebooks and Illustrative Programmes are not much help if you're looking for the safest places for it. Or for what to say to the police when they catch you. Or for where you can get a nice cup of tea after.

'Here, you started without us?'

'My brother had to go to the Infirmary with sand after Rhyl.'

The safest places, of course, are the beaches, where you can cram on top of each other, and press and rub away while

108

one-man bands and pierrots and donkeys step round you and pretend not to notice.

'All right, then, if you're going to you might as well.'

'What's this here? We got company?'

You'll not be worried too much in the shelters beyond the Shuttleworth Clock at the south end of South Bay. But how do you get someone to walk all that way to look at a clock saying two o'clock? And do you want to spend beano afternoon with them if they do?

'Go on!'

'All right then. I don't normally you know.'

You can of course try the slopes in the shadow of the castle on North Side, at the back of the new Floral Hall.

'Will here do?'

'It'll have to, look.'

But it's no good listing the best courting spots in Scarborough this last Friday afternoon. Mustard makes your beef taste nasty, when you don't put any on.

For the courting hour's started and we're too late to join in. Pretend we don't love anyone, and we are waiting for the paddling. And next year?

* * * * *

And Miss Tidmarsh and Mr Shephard, who love more than all Scarborough put together, are spending the courting hour in the photographers-to-royalty on the Spa.

When their turn comes, the photographer is most helpful.

Miss Tidmarsh is portrayed holding a parasol beside a rowing boat and a cloth backdrop of the sea.

And then Mr Shephard is photographed leaning on a gate in front of a field, holding a gun.

* * * * *

The sun glides out again and catches Spaldy eating a very late lunch up at the Castle. He has not stopped painting since the tide turned. He does not stop now, but munches a cold oatcake wrapped round a cold sausage with green tomato chutney in a parcel from his left hand, and stirs lemon yellow into raw umber and French ultramarine with his number four filbert brush, held in his right.

A courting couple tiptoe behind him, and nudge each other at his painting, or at his ambidexterity.

They sit with their banjo on their tartan rug, ten yards in front of him. Perhaps they settle there to nibble ears so they will be remembered on his oil painting as a permanent souvenir hanging in someone's home, with the sun blowing up a soft wind from the eternal sea in late July for ever. Perhaps they think that the artist can dull the pain of their separating love? And even stop time for a time?

Perhaps he can.

Bu he isn't doing.

For Spaldy goes on munching and painting, and does not offer to include the courting couple in either.

* * * * *

And Mr Holles splashes in the marble lavatories of the Grand Hotel and sings a complete song about a married man caught courting beside the seaside.

Poor Mrs Holles and the Girl wait in silence in the arched brick front of the Grand. They do not look at each other. They have not spoken all day.

* * * * *

And Mr Wagstaff comes out of the continuous performance of *The Sacrifice of Kathleen* at the Palladium, crosses the road, and takes the Tramway to Town. He walks for two minutes without looking up from the road, and goes into the Londsborough Picture House. He pays two shillings for a best seat, and goes into the dark to sit in it.

11

Out of Their Depth

The rusty-bums go for a swim – What Edna saw. And did –
Owen goes on an adventure – The lying Chapel party and
what Mr Holles tells them – Miss Tidmarsh and Mr Shephard
think about buying funeral jet – Tommy, Spud and Monkey go
for a run – And poor Mrs Holles gives a secret away.

> 'Finger thumb or
> Rusty bum?'

Tommy, Spud and Monkey are chanting and leapfrogging down the beach. Naked.

When at last they give Monkey a turn at the leapfrog Spud changes the game and becomes a rusty-bummed donkey trotting out to sea.

Rusty-bummed Monkey trots behind them down the beach, worrying about which leg should move with which, when donkeys trot. So when Tommy and Spud skid and stop, and curl up to cover themselves, Monkey cannot see and wobbles on past them. And so he is the one who runs naked into the policeman.

'Water-baby, are you?'

'Swimmin' mester.'

'You've no clothes on.'

'Nobody's looking, mester.'

'Ah, but there are by-laws.' The policeman puts his gloved hands on Monkey's bony shoulders. 'Now there are bathing vans and cubicles provided at intervals all along the four miles of our glorious beaches. Bathing drawers can readily be hired there.'

'No money, mester.'

'There are no by-laws about that.'

'Can you stop us, mester? It isn't your sea.'

The policeman strokes Monkey's bristly head. 'No, and I wouldn't swim in it if it was mine, either. Nasty, bad-tempered thing it is, the sea here. You should come back at Christmas and see what happens. If you follow those seagulls you'll see a pipe where all the sewage comes out in the summer. But you are right, I can't stop you swimming in it.'

'Good.'

'But I have to stop you swimming in it without your clothes on because of the by-laws. So come on and let's get you dressed.' He grins, and puts a gloved hand round Monkey's shoulders and leads him back up the beach to where the others are already struggling back into their clothes.

The policeman says nothing as he watches them all dress. They take a long time. He helps Monkey.

Tommy clutches the top of his trousers. 'We've come all this way for a swim, mister, and now we can't.'

'We can, Tommy,' Monkey says.

'Can't, mental!' Spud says. 'He's a copper.'

'Can, can't we mester? If we keep us clothes on?'

Tommy looks at the policeman. The policeman nods. Tommy decides as he always does, too fast for him to think.

'Right. Come on then, lads!' And he turns and dashes off to the sea still clutching his trousers and yelling, 'It's only what they do at the Baptists.'

He leads his converts right into the baptismal water, which is icy, even through your boots and your trousers, though the temperature's just over sixty and the warmest it will be all day. There's a hazy sunshine, and no wind.

The policeman at the sea's edge watches the three lads until they are well out of their depth.

* * * * *

But just beyond the Seamen's Bethel on Foreshore Road there is more undressing going on. Edna watches a man with no trousers chasing a young nun round an altar. A man with a moustache, too. The nun sticks her tongue out at him. He shakes his moustache. She dives under the altar. Underwear flies. And then she pokes up on the other side with bare shoulders. She tugs the altar cloth and drapes it over her. He stares, pop-eyed with lust, as a priest with a moustache pokes out of the cupboard.

And the light goes out.

'Let's get some fresh air,' Bess says. And indeed, the air is not at all fresh in this penny arcade full of machines.

Edna says, 'That were a poor ha'penny-worth. Never got nowhere.'

'You think of men and nowt else, Edna,' Ada says.

'Not my fault men like me. Did you see how that Mr Wilcock was pressing right into me at that café, and he didn't charge me for that last pot.'

'We reckon to be suffragettes.'

'We don't know owt about suffragettes, Ada.'

'We know we're wasting us holiday being pushed and shoved in here watching you on these daft machines.'

'They're not daft. "Push coin in slot. Then turn crank to right." Right. Me light's come on! Now if I crank right slow, I'll see each card as it flips over, like, and make it last. Oh, we're off. That's not allowed is it? You want to have a look, Bess?' But Edna keeps her eyes pressed deep into the binoculars of the Mutoscope machine.

'I'm going,' Bess says.

'Hey up,' Edna cries. 'Look what he's up to now, eh? And he's posh, too, just like all them others. Stiff collar. I'd say she's a tweeny, her, only she's lost most of her uniform before me light come on. Mind you, you never wore drawers like them when you was in service, Ada. He's got a touch of Mr Holles, he has. And she's seen him now. And she knows what's com—. Hello? Someone must have pinched some of the cards. It's happening on that settee. And she'll get lumbago doing that. Here, oh no, me light's gone now. I'm having another ha'porth. "Turn crank to right." '

'I'm going,' Bess says, pushing through the crowd.

'Me too, love,' Ada says.

'Just this one, Ada?' Edna drops her coin in. 'Bess is only being mardy cos she's not got a man at home waiting for her. Let her traipse off if she wants. You come and look at this muck with me.'

'Bye.'

'I'll not know where to meet you!'

'Expect you'll still be here being cockstruck.' And Ada is swallowed up in the crowds passing in front of the arcade.

Edna shrugs and looks back deep into the binoculars.

But twenty-five minutes of moustaches and underwear later she traipses out herself, rather flushed, and aiming for the harbour.

* * * * *

Owen in red tie and sandals shakes hands with the comrade from Manchester, in the summer dark of the main railway station opposite Mr Laughton's Pavilion Hotel.

'Next time we'll all look at the map,' the comrade grumbles from the train window. 'I've only just got here, and now I'm off again.'

'It was a good meeting mind you,' Owen says.

'Aye, and you'll now have a good afternoon to enjoy yourself in.'

'There's plenty of work to do here yet,' Owen says. But he blushes.

'You get yourself a boat and get off to Paris and make a bit of history.'

The comrade waves a clenched fist when the train chunters off, followed by a platoon of seagulls, who think it is a herring boat leaving on the tide.

Owen himself goes to the empty Third Class Waiting Room, and places leaflets on all the benches there.

As he comes out of the station he sees a survivor of Captain Scott's Antarctic expedition, begging. And speaks to him. For aren't we all victims of a heartless system that cares more for flags and minerals than it does for the sick and the exploited? He gives him a penny and a leaflet.

'You're a gent, sir,' Captain Scott's survivor says.

But look now at our revolutionary gent. See how deliberately he strides in his sandals down Westborough towards the harbour. And look at him go into that chocolate shop. He, who surely cannot believe in retailers?

'A half-pound of misshapes, please.'

'You do want the fancy box, of course, sir?'

And he does. Watch him striding back up towards the station and then left along Valley Bridge.

'One, please.'

'Yes, sir.'

And he who does not believe in private ownership pays a ha'penny toll to cross a bridge. And answers to 'sir'.

Look at him now as he strides up steep Ramshill Road, a hundred yards inland from the Esplanade and the sea.

Stopping now at the Church of St Martin-on-the-Hill on his right.

And he – who does not even believe in God – looks round, quickly, and goes in!

Chocolates in fancy boxes? Tolls? Churches? He'll be getting married next.

* * * * *

'On Jordan's stormy banks I stand', the Chapel folk lie, for in fact they stand on South Sands, helping at the Revival meeting that's held here every courting hour to try and stop it.

> 'And cast a wistful eye
> To Canaan's fair and happy land,
> Where my possessions lie.'

* * * * *

Mr Holles purchases an evening newspaper, and steers his women over Foreshore Road to the hymn-singing Chapel folk. The Chapel folk notice him and wave towards him without stopping singing.

> 'Though Jordan's waves around me roll
> Fearless I would launch away.'

Mr Holles is invited into the roped-off area on the sands to give them an address.

He steps inside, and refuses. 'I am the biggest sinner in Scarborough. In the whole of Yorkshire from the Derwent to the Don. God only knows how much I can sin when I want to. So I'm not the man to address you on sin. But I'll say this to you as a brewer. You teetotallers are a disgrace. Everyone knows that Jesus drank wine after his full day's work at his carpentry. He even did some brewing at Cana at that wedding. You teetotallers might make good workers up to foreman level. And good timekeepers. And, like Jesus, you might be against so-called trade unionitis of course. But you are no company for a grown sinner like me. Take poor Mrs Holles's father, he was a teetotaller. It didn't stop him going bankrupt and having to sell his daughter to me before he died. He brought poor Mrs Holles here when she was a lass, took her on a long wooden pier and made her cry before he carried her back wrapped up in his waistcoat. Oh, she remembers it all very clearly. She's been going round telling flunkeys about it all day. The only trouble is she remembers it all wrong. And that's teetotalism for you! Now then, we're just off to the harbour again. I've heard there's four piers down there, so she can have a cry on one of them while I take the Girl here on a double bicycle round the Marine Drive.' He nods at the Chapel folk. 'God bless us all. And let's hear some good singing to discourage those younger sinners who are out in the bushes taking their clothes off.' And he bows. And calls, 'Amen.'

'Amen,' call the congregation. And there are twice as many of them now as there were when he started.

The Chapel folk raise their hats in thanks.

Mr Holles gooses the Girl and steers her towards the harbour. Mrs Holles flutters behind.

* * * * *

' "Queen Victoria made Whitby jet very fashionable in the early years of her widowhood after the death of her beloved Albert." ' Mr Shephard looks up from his guidebook.

Miss Tidmarsh and he are in the Spa Jewellers looking at funeral jewellery.

They finger jet brooches, jet necklaces, jet bangles and jet rings.

'Miss Tidmarsh, I hope you would not be offended if I said I would like you to allow me to purchase you a present of a trinket in Whitby jet as a souvenir of this day.'

'No – thank you, Trevor. But no.'

'I quite understand. I should not have asked. Perhaps we should be wending our way to the Pump Room and then the concert, anyway?'

The sun is shining white above the churning sea outside. But Miss Tidmarsh begins to shiver and cannot stop. They join the small queue of invalids waiting to drink the spa water.

* * * * *

Tommy, Monkey and Spud are shivering in a queue waiting

for the long tram ride back from Peasholm to Foreshore Road where Monkey begged his miracle this morning.

They shiver at the bottom of Columbus Ravine as three trams fill up. When they get on the platform of the fourth to go inside where it should be warmer the conductor at the bottom of the curly steps shakes his head. 'You tykes aren't coming on. You're soaking wet. There are the other passengers. And there are the by-laws.'

Monkey says, 'Please, mester? We're frozen. We had to swim with us clothes on, mester. Cos of the by-laws, mester.'

'He's mental, mister, just take us two and leave him.'

'Off!'

Spud says, 'Cough.' He kicks the conductor's leather bag. Coins fountain everywhere. 'Go on, cough!'

Tommy grabs the ticket rack and sprays tickets at the queue. 'Come on, tykes!' Tommy shouts and tears off, tugging at his trousers, down to the sea. Spud and Monkey tear after him.

They race along flat Royal Albert Drive, with the churning sea on their left, as the courting hour ends, and the discreet sun comes out again.

'Come on, tykes!'

They tear on though no one is chasing them now. They go under Clarence Gardens with its flagpoles and hillocks and bandstand and bowls and tennis.

They run on over a mile now, going faster if anything, as Royal Albert Drive swerves out to sea. They laugh and spit. It is much more fun than anything they have done all day.

'Run right round to that other sea?'

'Yeah, Tommy!'

They run on below a second packed bowling green, and towards the crumbling yellow cliffs where the seagulls muster and burp after lunch.

The tide is already up here, sloshing the bottom of the sea wall. In unison they dodge the afternoon promenaders who have not needed the full hour for their courting, because they were too old. Or married. Or quick.

'Can run for ever, me!' Tommy calls.

'I can and all, Tommy.'

But they cannot.

For there are two red-brick houses and a toll barrier now where Royal Albert Drive changes colour to become the new Marine Drive.

And there is a notice that begins 'Every person on foot 1*d*; on horseback 1*d*; on bicycle (other than motor cycle) 1*d*; every person in any carriage, motor car, bath chair or other vehicle 1*d*'.

'Come on, tykes!'

They leap the toll barrier and swerve past a family in fur coats who have almost had their pennyworths coming the other way. Past the wobbling landlady of the Britlings pub by the cemetery straddling a horse. She waves, mistaking them for nice young lads from home.

But then three men in peaked caps grab them. Hurt them. And turn them round.

And they still run, back the way they came now, shrieking and swearing.

'Cough!'

'Come on, tykes!'

Tommy leads them up on to the bowling green. He stumbles on its softness, clutches at his trousers and then seems almost to dance as he feels the grass under his sodden boots. Spud and Monkey run on after him. Spud fires a cluster of bowls at the ankles of two old men and hits them. The bowlers curse the times, and the young people who are inheriting them. But they are too old for it to be much fun here.

'Cough! Cough!'

'Come on, you tykes.'

Tommy runs, leading the stowaways beyond the bowls and up along the winding path to the tennis courts. Here Spud catches the balls and throws them high down on to Royal Albert Drive for the fur-coated family striding on doing themselves good. Tommy kicks the net and winds it down. Spud grabs a woman's racquet and stamps through its strings.

Tennis is much more fun than bowls, for the tennis players bend and swerve and line up to blockade the tykes. But even they are too slow. Spud lifts a woman player's dress with a broken racquet while Tommy pinches her purse. He fences a man in a blazer who smells of candle and wants to thrash him with his cane.

'Cough, you!'

'Come on, tykes!'

They chase on up the winding paths. Spud steals a cigarette from two emancipated women reading a Fabian pamphlet on a bench.

A woman is singing opera in a small bandstand. Spud lifts the back arm of a parson's deckchair to wake him up so he does not miss it. But he does, for he smashes his head on the paving stones.

'Come on, you tykes!'

'Cough, all of you, eh!'

They run up the paths to Queen's Arcade, past Gibsons and the other North Bay hotels with sea views beyond Scalby. And then they dash back on to the tilting paths that wind up over the broken back of Scarborough. There are a few courting couples here, apologizing. The tykes grunt past them, and on up right to the Castle.

Tommy gasps, 'In here, tykes!'

'Threepence each, Tom!' Spud groans.

'Purse – look!' Tommy holds up a woman's purse. He tips the coins into his hands – all silver and all big. He throws the purse itself down among the thick courting bushes on the yellow hillside.

The tykes shuffle up the queue at the Castle entrance. Monkey's teeth are chattering even when he clenches them till they hurt. Their clothes rub and their boots squelch.

'Champion, eh?' Tommy stares. 'Nearly lost me trousers at that tennis court.' And then, 'Three tickets for the Castle, please mester.'

And the man in the box says, 'Certainly, sir.'

Tommy grins at that, too. Murmurs to Spud, 'Never been called "sir" afore.' He must be growing up. (A dangerous thing to be doing this year, mind you.)

They stumble up the cobbled hill to the broken keep, and beyond to the great open grassland.

'How much we pinch, Tommy?'

'Quids. Best hide for a bit.' He marches them on to a grass mound. They take off their boots and line them up like the

Baptists do. 'God knows what Jesus'll think about it, mind you. He don't believe in stealing.'

There is a courting couple wrapped up together with a banjo twenty yards off. Spud shuffles towards the woman's handbag just as Spaldy, still painting, looks up and waves with his stumpy pipe. 'Now then, Monkey, you scallybrat. Enjoying your beano?'

'King champion, mester!'

'Come here,' Spaldy calls. 'What do you think of me picture?'

'It's all wet, mester.'

Spaldy gives him a penny for spice and carries on painting.

Tommy says, 'Funny, isn't it, my trousers have stopped squeaking.' And he adds, 'We'll have five minutes' rest like soldiers do every hour when they march. You're on guard, Monkey.'

'Yes, sir.' Monkey salutes.

Tommy and Spud lie on their backs in the grass. And sleep in the sunshine.

Monkey stands to attention, with one hand in his holey pocket, and stares at the Castle. Who brought all the stones up here to build it? And why did they want a castle up here anyway? Who would want this crumbling hill?

* * * * *

And just below that hill, at twenty-past three, see poor Mrs Holles on an empty public bench in front of the fish sellers' booths by the lifeboat.

And watch now as a woman with a brown parcel sits down at the other end and licks a pencil stub. Mrs Holles looks at her, wonders how old she is and why she too is alone here this Scarborough afternoon.

The woman looks up. Covers the parcel. Smiles. Is about to speak. But Mrs Holles speaks first. 'I'm looking for a wooden pier. You don't know where there is a wooden pier, do you?'

'No, I'm sorry.'

'I've lost it you see.'

'Oh dear. On your own, are you?' And the woman looks worried about her. No one has worried about poor Mrs Holles for so long. She thinks she will cry.

'I'm with my husband. But he has gone for a bicycle ride

with the maid. He is going to have connection with her tonight.'

'Oh?'

'My husband is not a nice man, I'm afraid.'

'Isn't he?'

'Can I tell you?' Mrs Holles slides along the bench.

'If you think you should. I've had my own troubles,' the woman says. And adds, 'And I'm a suffragette now, of course.'

'Are you?'

'For today, like.'

'My husband says I can't remember things. But when I was young . . .' And poor Mrs Holles talks for twenty minutes about the wooden pier. And her father. And Mr Holles, of course.

The woman nods or shakes her head or grunts all the time, and seems very understanding.

Mrs Holles finishes. 'I'm so sorry to burden you with my troubles. But I had to tell somebody.'

'"Course you did.'

'It's easier talking to a stranger.'

'And a suffragette. I mean as a suffragette I do have some idea about what men are like, see. I've studied some conjugal cases. And yours does *that* to you, doesn't he? With you being – you know?'

'Do you think I should join the suffragettes?'

'Don't see why not. It does you good sometimes.'

They lean back, side by side in the middle of the bench. Poor Mrs Holles smells fish from the woman's brown paper parcel, and frowns, and knows she is going mad again.

The woman licks her pencil stub and says, 'Aye well, eh.' She begins to write, in big slow letters, a man's name.

And Mr Holles arrives, flushed and bursting out of his beano suit, followed by the Girl, looking plumper than ever. Mr Holles calls, 'Still here getting bilious about your lost happiness, Missis? Hello, hello – I know you, don't I?'

'Yes, sir,' the woman with the parcel says, standing up to curtsy.

'Don't tell me. You listen to this, Girl, and you'll see how your memory can work. This woman here with the parcel has a pretty head on her, hasn't she? "Head on her" – "Ed on er" – she's Ed-on-er from Bottles, aren't you?'

'Yes Mr Holles, sir.'

Poor Mrs Holles stares at Edna. From bottles? Unrecognizable in her beano clothes, of course, even if Mrs Holles had ever been in the brewery bottling room and had seen her. But one of the employees she has been telling tales to. All the most secret things about Mr Holles.

Mr Holles says, 'Well, Ed-on-er, and who are you writing to?'

'It's a boneless kipper for the post, sir.'

'Who's it for, though? Not your husband or you'd be taking it home with you.'

'He's a relative, sir. A cousin.'

'Happen. I don't expect it'll stop him slipping something boneless to you in return for the fish. And have you been having a nice chat with poor Mrs Holles, Ed-on-er?'

'Yes, sir.'

'She been telling you all about the wooden pier she remembers so clearly from her happy childhood that turns out to be untrue?'

'Sir.'

'And about how bilious she is?'

'Sir,' Edna says. (But she does not add 'and why'.)

'Well, we're off to take the spa waters for that biliousness. That or Zam Buk. Ever been on a double boneshaker, Ed-on-er? I'll show you. You drive, Girl. Gee up.'

'Sir.' And he straddles an imaginary tandem behind the Girl, and rubs and jumps and rides her off down the front.

Poor Mrs Holles trots after them without looking at Edna again.

Edna licks her stamp and places it on the parcel of boneless kipper very deliberately, and takes it back to the stall to be posted there.

* * * * *

And there are just over three hours to the beano photograph now. Edna will not be on it at all, of course. But poor Mrs Holles will – smiling! And what will she have to smile about in three hours' time, that she is not smiling about now?

PART FIVE

12

Free For All

*Cherrywood pipes and chocolate – William Morris speaks to
Owen – A great money trick – Oatcakes or revolution?*

'Bye-bye then, you bugger.'

Ten to four, and the ancient blacksmith stands by the
lighthouse looking into the rising waters at the harbour. The
fish and seaweed and ozone smell wonderful.

From his waistcoat pocket he takes his blocked pipe. He
snaps it and drops it into the North Sea.

He then chunters back up the pier past all the excursionists
and fisherfolk, and a man cutting up potatoes to sell a knife
that is always sharp, and a professor playing a piano with a
dog sitting on it, and several women doing eurhythmics, and
a sad sand-sculptor, and a nigger minstrel demonstrating the
diabolo.

He chunters along Sandside and up Eastborough and
Westborough, past a drapers, and goes into the tiny tobac-
conist there that smells, even from the noisy street, like
tobacconists used to smell when he was a child and his father
used to let him rub the Robin Flakes warm in his palms.

He buys a cherrywood pipe and chunters back out and
down to the sea. But he stops outside a chocolate shop and
breathes it in.

* * * * *

And Owen is still clutching his fancy box of misshapes he
bought at that same shop, alone in the Lady Chapel of St
Martin-on-the-Hill. Nodding – at John the Baptist. And talking to himself.

'Not been inside a church for twenty years. Never going in

again if I can help it!' John the Baptist! . . . The voice crying in the wilderness . . . Mary Magdalene, the exploited woman who wanted all women to see their exploitation . . . And the prophet Isaiah telling corrupt Judah to change – not the sin-sodden people from Owen's growing-up when God was alive and distracting you. But John and the Magdalene and Isaiah are human, sinless workers in bright colours among English greens and spring flowers and real tools for real labour.

Owen talks to himself. 'I told Flossie this morning. We are everywhere, even in this sternest corner of respectable Scarborough, where they build churches for themselves to celebrate their robbery in every Sunday. But they're so ignorant, though they are cruel with all their privilege and wealth. They asked a revolutionary to make their windows for them! And William Morris touched this revolutionary glass and lead.'

And it is true. William Morris and the firm began to fill dour St Martin's with pre-Raphaelite glass and cloth and wood and paint and light in 1862. The firm was only two years old then, and Morris only twenty-eight. The church itself was finished in 1861 and has been described since as 'confused and uninspired', with a French feel about it. G. F. Bodley was the confused, uninspired designer. The South Cliff Company gave the land. And a rich spinster, Mary Craven, paid for it. And it opened two months late because there were such quarrels among the respectable thieves about how much rent they should pay for their pews . . .

Owen knows little of this, though he could guess most of it. He doesn't care about it as he touches the exhibits in this most unexpected art gallery in England, all angels playing bagpipes, and roses and harebells and forget-me-nots – and martins on the wing everywhere, for St *Martin*-on-the-Hill!

'We are everywhere, just as I told Flossie. Each Sunday morning when they kneel here to thank their dead god for giving them more than their share for doing less than their share, all this laughs at them! And things won't always be so! For they are already changing – look! The alchemy of socialism! All these flowers and springtime! From altar to roof in glass and stone and wood and light!

'All this fun! Made by men who've found their world ugly and started to change it, by just looking at it in a different way! For once you can see how things can be different, they can be! Even here in the very museums of privilege that can be decorated by William Morris and sing of hope and change. All change! Silence the brass bands! It is coming!

'William Morris was here and his comrades!' Owen is shouting now in the empty church, and his voice is strong. 'Burne-Jones and Ford Madox Brown and Dante Gabriel Rossetti! On every stained glass and wall and altar and pulpit and roof, wherever there is space to be beautiful even in this ugliest of times – democracy! And beautiful workers and draughtsmen from before and after the factories! When everyone who works is beautiful and equal, and there are no cripples, no smoke and no despair. I am not alone! Morris is dead! I will be dead! But what we say stays true – look at it! Listen! "If others can see it as I have seen it then it may be called a vision rather than a dream".'

Owen slaps his copy of Morris's *News from Nowhere*. He does not need to check the last sentence of that book. He goes to work instead.

It takes him twenty minutes as the sun flares from William Morris's John the Baptist, all bright green and light, to fold most of his remaining leaflets into all the prayer books ready for Sunday.

The future can be changed. It is coming!

* * * * *

But listen. A hundred yards nearer the sea, Mr Holles is dribbling five gold sovereigns into his straw hat, at the Esplanade entrance to the Spa. He is watched by poor Mrs Holles, the Girl, and twenty-three strangers and a fat dog.

'Five.' And in one quick throw he snaps his hat and the sovereigns on to his head.

He holds both empty palms at his applauding crowd. 'Now I have promised to give you five gold sovereigns. But first you must listen to a short scientific speech about political economy. If your business on the Spa is too urgent, please pay your own ninepences and go in.'

Nobody does.

And nobody looks at the sea through the lush Spa trees. It's halfway up the sands now and frothing and squeezing into South Bay. You can hear its growl even up here where the more fashionable folks stroll to discuss the Roses match and tea, when not distracted by the chance of something for nothing, scientific or not.

Mr Holles speaks again. 'My name's Holles. I make Britlings beer. My father made it. My father's father made it. And Britlings is best. This is my beano suit which you will agree is amazing.'

Some applause. The speech is finished. Long live the philanthropist.

But the speech is not finished.

'That is the poor Mrs Holles. She thinks she came to Scarborough as a child with her teetotal father. This is my Girl and her watch is gold.'

Applause. It has been most interesting. Long live poor Mrs Holles, the Girl and gold.

'Now poor Mrs Holles will not approve of what I am about to do. But if I were to do the only thing that Mrs Holles would approve of I would – ah-aaaaaaah!'

And he has a massive heart attack and falls to the ground dead.

Mrs Holles's prayers have come true. She can believe in God and the triumph over evil again. For a moment.

Mr Holles springs up daintily and bows. 'Sorry, Mrs Holles.'

Applause. What a card, eh? Giving away gold. With his light mahogany voice like a Spa singer's? Rising from the dead to annoy his poor wife.

'Now poor Mrs Holles is a Liberal. Such money as she had came from her teetotal family's land. She herself prefers money to be conjured for her by workers she cannot see in distant summery cornfields. For the trouble with money from brewing is that you have to see the workers you daily sparge. You even have to come on holiday with them.'

Applause. Long live holidays! And the end of the speech!

Mr Holles senses a desire for his speech to stop. He lifts his boater. The crowd expect the coins to shower down from his head. But they do not.

What conjuring! For when he opens his big left fist – the gold is now safely cupped there!

Big applause for that as he dribbles and clicks the coins back into his straw hat in the golden afternoon.

'Now Mrs Holles thinks my money should be distributed more fairly, so that people who cannot conjure gold like I can conjure gold should be given mine. She thinks her Mr Lloyd George should tax it and give it to his unemployed and sick. Thus.'

Mr Holles plunges his fist into the hat, pulls out a sovereign and flings it into the yellow roses twenty yards away.

The crowd even hear it fall.

And a boy in a sailor suit even runs after it, followed by the barking dog. And they scar and tear themselves in the rose bushes. But look now, and you'll see Mr Holles open his right fist, to count up all five coins, still safely there!

The crowds laugh. They do not call the sailor boy or the fat dog back from the roses. Mr Holles is not surprised.

He speaks more softly. 'As you can see I do not believe in throwing my money away. I believe in work and making work for others.' He beckons the Girl. The crowd take note of her tight uniform, her plumpness, and her gold watch. She curtsies.

'You're seventeen, aren't you, Girl?'

'Sir.'

'You left the institution when you were thirteen. What have you done since then?'

'I looked after a lady, sir, till she died. Then I had nobody, sir. Until the church, sir, found me a good position with you at The Lawns five months ago, thank you, sir. Sir.'

Mr Holles pats her. He looks up at his audience. 'And so this orphan now has a home. A "good position" she is good enough to call it. Certainly she eats the same food I eat. She sleeps in my beds. She comes on my holidays. Did taxes do that for her?'

'No!'

'No! If I allow any more of my conjured money to be stolen in tax and given to Mr Lloyd George's workless I shall have none for wages, shall I? So she will have no home again. No food. No holidays. No work! She will have to walk the streets.' He strokes her neck. 'Now, no doubt you are saying that she's a fine-looking girl well able with her dark gypsy looks to earn enough money for a few degrading years by walking the streets of Whitby.' He pushes her away. 'No, for if Mrs Holles has her way, which of us men will have pocket money left for whoring after what we earn from our conjuring and alchemy has been stolen and given to the workless who neither conjure nor alchemize?'

And he shows his hat and his hands. And all the money has gone.

He turns away and the crowd roars as he conjures coins from the Scarborough air. 'Then don't vote for Mrs Holles and Mr Lloyd George! I have warned you.' And he dribbles the coins into his hat.

The crowds cheer. Long live the whores of Whitby, and Mrs Holles, and Mr Holles, of course, who is now saying, 'This town in the past has sent a Liberal MP to London. Which shows great gratitude I must say. And I will say this, too, if in my town there were ever to be a Liberal Member of Parliament I should take down my brewery brick by brick and build it somewhere more grateful with a better sense of political economy.' The crowds applaud. Long live political economy.

'Now if I were a brewery worker, of course,' Mr Holles adds, for even now he's not had his twenty-three pounds worth, 'and I was sparged every day by political economy that worked me so hard but paid me only just as much as I needed to be fit for work each day, then I should not think as I do now. But I wouldn't be a Liberal. Look!'

For he now chews and swallows the gold coins, to demonstrate how the Liberals force the sick, old and unemployed to eat the wealth of the nation. They do not go to public houses to buy beer, do they, so less beer is produced, so brewery workers lose their jobs. So they spend less on beer. So less beer is produced. So more brewery workers lose their jobs. So . . .

Mr Holles swallows the fifth gold coin and opens his empty mouth to prove it. Then he holds out his straw hat, puts in his hand, and plucks out – the five gold coins.

Applause. What a card! He must surely be finished by now?

Mr Holles says he must rush now, and explains why he's giving his sovereigns to the queue.

It is not because they are sick and old and unemployed.

It is because they are *not* sick and old and unemployed. For they will not eat the wealth, will they? They will spend it. And every time a coin is spent work is created. When there is more work there is more spending. Thus other workers get more work. Soon each household is earning again and can choose whether or not to spend their own money on their own sick and old. Political economy. For soon enough we shall all have the choice of working hard and spending hard on Britlings beer and Whitby whores for ever.

Applause.

Mr Holles invites them to come to his hat for a gold coin. All they must do is promise not to keep it till the morning.

The crowd shuffles, not sure if this is another trick, and another false ending.

It is.

Mr Holles says, 'Oh, if you see any sparged Britlings Brewery workers on their beano today please tell them you met Mr Holles. Explain to them why they must drink as much Britlings beer as they can today, if they want a job next week. Tell them to vote Conservative too, if you wish, though they already do, like every landlord in every pub you've ever been in.'

He turns his hat upside down and walks away as if, this time, he does not even realize where the gold coins are. Down they tumble and roll all over the path. He does not wait to see the fight that follows. He knows there will be a fight. Isn't that why he's a Conservative? Besides, it does not matter as long as the money is spent.

He puts an arm round the Girl and poor Mrs Holles, and sweeps them into the Spa, without paying.

* * * * *

Owen pads down past the Esplanade entrance to the Spa just as the yelling crowd fights for Mr Holles's five gold coins. He assumes their high spirits come from their being so prosperous in an unequal world that is about to change. But how to change it? And at what cost to yourself? He does not see Mr Holles who, unlike him, has never found his politics ever need contradict his urge for enjoyment.

Never mind, it's all going to change, isn't it?

And Owen is singing as he pads past the Spa entrance in the Esplanade and down towards the steps to the harbour.

* * * * *

The waves are getting higher. The waxing tide seems to be doing strange things to people.

If the fortune-tellers had not gone we could ask them if the tides do affect us? Or if there is something else that we should know?

13

Lovers

*The taste of the Spa – A proposal – The composer Meyerbeer,
his name and music, followed by Sir Arthur Sullivan –
Surprise music lovers – The shooting of the sausage – And
what happened after – The vulgar wasp.*

Just after twenty-past three, and Miss Tidmarsh and Mr
Shephard take the spa water in the damp Pump Room. They
take it aerated and warm at a penny a glass.

He tastes blood. She smells dust and medicine.

But they do not say so.

* * * * *

'Sit still.'

'I am. It's you.'

Percy is paddling Lizzie on a canoe in Peasholm Park
around the Japanese Lake. She sits in front, facing the water.
He sits at the back with the paddle, swearing each time his
collar scrapes his neck.

'Come on, Percy, let's get going.'

'You're too fat.'

(If you are a fat member of the House of Commons and you
wish to resign your seat but a fatter MP has already applied
for the stewardship of the Chiltern Hundreds before you, you
can apply for the stewardship of the Manor of Northstead. If
you do, you will for a time be steward of this Peasholm Park,
in charge of the large ornamental boating lake and several
other smaller lakes and ponds totalling almost five acres.
There are two islands, some fish, many ducks trailing their
families, especially in July, and many things Japanese –
including the Japanese Bridge, the Japanese Waterfall, the

Japanese Shelter, and the beginnings of the Japanese Forest rising up out of the steep ravine from the valley. In fact few MPs come here, for Peasholm Park is on the North Side and newly created for the new kind of excursionist.)

It's sixpence per person per hour on the canoes. And they are not easy.

'King canoes!'

'You were the one what wanted to come boating, Perce.'

'Not with you,' he shouts at her back.

Lizzie trickles her fingers. 'I wouldn't muck you about like Bunty.'

'I'm trying to chuffing steer.'

But he is not trying chuffing hard enough. He smacks the prow into the middle leg of the rainbow Japanese Bridge that Miss Tidmarsh almost sent to her father this morning. Lizzie jerks and chops. He does not apologize. She does not look round.

He paddles and pokes until the canoe is horizontal in the narrow waterway, causing other couples to hit each other. At last he makes a dash for the bridge, and shoots out into the widest part of the lake, almost under the Japanese Waterfall. He swears and stops paddling. 'I'm going round her mum's first thing tomorrow to find out what she's reckoned to be poorly with.'

'She's not reckoned to be poorly.'

'What do you know about it?'

'I were round her house last night to curl her hair.'

'For the beano?'

'Course.'

'So she's poorly. You're daft, you, Lizzie. Daft as you look.' He bonks the Japanese Bandstand with the canoe side.

Lizzie does not turn round. 'You look all right, you. Specially your bum.'

'Give over.'

'Always on about your bum, Bunty were.'

'She loves me.'

'Doesn't.'

'She told me.'

'Once. That Friday you gave her that brooch and got that nosebleed.'

134

He stops paddling.

And Lizzie does turn round now, and looks at him. He is all grimy from the train, and red-necked, and wet from the canoe, in his shirt sleeves. She crawls, rocking towards him.

'You'll have us over.'

She kneels, facing him from the middle of the canoe. 'I like your bum as much as anyone. I don't mind nosebleeds.'

'Sit down, will you?'

'I can do owt Bunty can do. And a few things she's too mardy to do.'

'You can't look like her, Lizzie.'

'And you can keep your eyes shut.' A mother duck and seven tiny soft ducklings splash towards the stationary canoe. 'And I know what I look like, Percy, so you don't have to keep saying. Besides.' The duck family is so close you could stroke them. 'I might start looking a bit better if some prince or something kissed me now and then. No wonder I look like a frog.'

'First sensible thing you've said all day.'

She hops towards him. 'Croak.'

'Stop it, daft, you'll sink us both.'

'Croak.'

'There's a deposit.'

'Kiss after then?' She clutches his knee.

His face is as red as his neck. He has never looked at her like this before.

'You can do me as well, Percy?'

'Eh?'

'Do me? Will you?'

She sits on the wet board between his knees, and he paddles one last wobbly circuit, without speaking. A lad with a hook stick has to wade out in high wellingtons to land the canoe. He says they are not sitting right and they are not allowed. But Percy gets his deposit back.

Lizzie says, 'Up there might be a bit private?' And as they climb up from the Japanese Lake to the newly planted Japanese Forest she says, 'Sign of a hard winter mind you, Percy, when the hay begins to run after the horse?'

* * * * *

Quarter to four, and Miss Tidmarsh and Mr Shephard in

135

touching wooden chairs at the front of the forecourt join in the applause for Mr Alick Maclean's Spa Orchestra's performance of the Coronation March from Giacomo Meyerbeer's *Prophet*.

There are twenty-nine perspiring musicians squeezed into the bandstand, not counting Mr Maclean himself, standing out in the July open air as the sea rolls into the two bays of Scarborough. The sun is almost clouded over but Sir Edwin Cooper's golden globe still shimmers above the new bandstand that holds the heat this afternoon.

And the orchestra is trussed up in suits and stiff collars, and they perspire. They have many moustaches, too. Indeed, if Edna from Washing were ever to come on the Spa – and she will not, at ninepence a session – she would be comforted by the survival of the moustache here, even among the younger men. She would not be the only deckchaired music lover who would sit through the concerts counting the sixteen moustaches on show. Or guessing Mr Maclean's height (six feet six, surely?)

Huge Mr Maclean himself stands just outside the bandstand, aloof and aristocratic, and huge enough not to need a moustache to keep order in the marble forecourt, or beyond it, on all the levels of Sir Joseph Paxton's Italian terraces and stern symmetrical walls and flights of pantomime stairs. Or beyond even all that on the paths that meander between the steep clipped lawns and respectful trees, a hundred feet and more to the Esplanade, where you do not even have to pay to hear the music but where you are expected to applaud like everyone else – and to stand up for the Anthem at the end.

Miss Tidmarsh leans now, during the applause for Giacomo Meyerbeer's Coronation March, and speaks sideways to Mr Shephard who has been resting his eyes. 'I believe Giacomo Meyerbeer's real name was Giacomo Beer, Trevor. But he inherited a certain sum of money from a relative named Meyer and so changed himself.'

'I suppose Beer is not quite the name for a composer. It does perhaps more suit – a brewer?'

'And later in life he took twenty-five years to write his opera *L'Africain*, but then died while rehearsing it, before it was even performed.'

Mr Maclean taps his baton and surveys his horizontal and vertical audiences. He speaks briefly of the advantage of the cornet, and explains why it has now permanently replaced the trumpet in the concert orchestra. He speaks with absolute certainty. (But if you cannot be absolutely certain on the Spa at Scarborough on a July afternoon then where can you be?)

He speaks briefly, next, of Sir Arthur Sullivan and his permanent reputation as a serious composer in spite of the comic operas. He speaks of Sir Arthur's masterpiece, 'The Lost Chord'. He demonstrates its unexpected musical structure and briefly muses on the words which, he says, uncannily catch that sense of certain hope we all feel at our most dejected, though the certainty and the hope soon fade, and leave us with only the faintest taste to sustain us. But we shall all perhaps hear that 'sound of a great amen' once more, shall we not?

Miss Tidmarsh shivers.

Mr Maclean now asks his audience's gracious permission to reintroduce this week's specially engaged artist, the celebrated European cornet player, Herr Vincent Bach.

And the celebrated Herr Bach walks briskly from the glass tea room and through the deckchaired audience, with a neat gold cornet that lobs the sun back up to Sir Edwin's globe, and then on up into the white July sky.

The celebrated Herr Bach is a very square man, all square spectacles, square shoulders and white square shoes. Even his cornet is square, and convenient, no doubt, for commuting from Europe to where he is especially engaged to play to seaside audiences all the English summer.

Miss Tidmarsh looks at Mr Shephard and sees that he is asleep by her side. She has never seen him sleep.

The afternoon smells of warm geraniums and cake. She rests her gloved hand on his arm. Under the glove, of course, is her dead mother's ring.

And Mr Maclean taps his baton for 'The Lost Chord'.

* * * * *

Albert and Flossie are also on the Spa, searching for the free music.

Mind you, it's already cost them ninepence each to come on the Spa, but Flossie fancied the spa water to settle the beer. And you do only come to Scarborough once, don't you? So they've drunk the fizzy water on the Spa, and it tasted of old lino. It does not seem to be doing them any good at all as they arm-in-arm and fizz through the fashionable crowds to where the music's being given away.

'Love tunes, always have, Albie.'

'Aye, well.'

They push past the sitting promenaders along the sea wall, safely above the trippers and the invading sea. And they reach Mr Maclean's main deckchaired audience just as 'The Lost Chord' starts.

'Sad, eh?'

'Oh aye, well, it's meant to be.'

Albert staggers and bumps into a fat man in a deckchair who was dreaming he was safe at an orchestral concert on the Spa at Scarborough on a sunny July afternoon.

'Soz me old. Whoops.' Albert staggers the other way and sits on a thin chaperon who is playing clock Patience on her lap with very tiny cards.

'It's all right, love,' Flossie calls, 'but he's just potted-up, been boozing since we set out, see.'

Herr Vincent Bach begins his solo. And the afternoon is even sadder. If there is certain hope, like Mr Maclean promised, there is not much.

Flossie winks at a deckchaired woman crocheting in rhythm for Christmas. 'All right then, are we, love?'

Albert says, ' "Ah love! Let us be true to one another. For the world what seems to lie before us like a land – ''. '

'Ssh Albie. They're listening to the tunes.'

'And I'm doing them a bit of Matthew Arnold to go with them.' He grabs Flossie's arm. ' "Land of dreams"!' He pushes Flossie away and turns to embrace the deckchaired audience. He opens his arms to enclose all friends of Mr Matthew Arnold, and sadness, and recites in his biggest voice ever, ' "For the world what seems to lie before us like a land of dreams so various so beautiful so new hath neither joy nor love nor pain nor light nor" – you'll like this, Flossie! – "certitude." Eh?'

Herr Bach is louder than he was. But too many of his audience are now listening to Albert yelling, ' "Here on a darkling plain swept by confused alarms, ignorant armies clash by night." '

Flossie breathes beer and spa water on to the crocheting woman. 'He works at a brewery, see, so he's got to drink, bless him.'

Albert snaps round. 'Your life goes too fast! Longer you carry on, faster it goes. Like your holiday. And it doesn't mean nothing.'

Herr Bach stops playing. Mr Maclean beaches the orchestra.

'They reckon you're drunk, Albie.'

'Aye, good old Britlings!'

* * * * *

Britlings!

Miss Tidmarsh hears. She grips Mr Shephard and he wakes to see her staring in terror. And notices her hand on his arm.

* * * * *

As Albert yells, ' "I hear it all by the distant northern sea!" '

'See?' says Flossie, and his cap falls off.

'Is this a "land of dreams" then? Not where we come from, it's not. It's all smoke and stink, making your beer for you.'

'They reckon you're spoiling the tunes, Albie.'

'Where's the tunes in our lives?'

Flossie bends to whisper to the crochet woman.

'I'm talking about us lives.' Albert is very angry. 'Mr Matthew Arnold would have understood. It's only just coming back to me today, but by God it's right. We are all stuck here on a darkling plain. Thing is,' he shakes his head, 'I don't know what "darkling" is, see.'

'Wait a moment, wait a mo!' Flossie shouts. 'This kind lady doing this knitting here tells me he's German.'

'Matthew Arnold?'

'Him. Herr Vincent Bach. He's a sausage. "Herr" means "mester" in their language. And if he's a German I'm going to shoot him. Get in there first.' Flossie kneels, frowns along his outstretched arm, and shoots. 'I told Owensie it's coming. Bang-bang, you're dead, Fritzie!'

And Flossie stands up waving his gun arm to the crowd to

applaud. And sees two people he knows. 'Here! Remember that snotty couple from Accounts we saw up on that bridge this morning? That's Miss –'

* * * * *

Miss Tidmarsh turns to bury her face in Mr Shephard's hot coat. But his deckchair slides, flinging her and then him on to the enclosure's new checked floor.

* * * * *

And Albert and Flossie are arrested by a young policeman who says he doesn't want any unpleasantness.

Flossie says he was not really shooting Fritzie. He likes tunes as much as the next man, but he's a patriot who'll fight for his country first. Long live King Edward the Peacemaker!

Albert asks the policeman what 'darkling' is.

The policeman says he thinks King Edward died but he does not know what 'darkling' is.

Flossie says he's well known at Britlings Brewery. But when he turns to point out two of his staff who can vouch for him, the snotty couple aren't there!

And the policeman takes each brewer by the elbow, and leads them off for a refund.

* * * * *

And, lying among the collapsed deckchairs, Mr Shephard and Miss Tidmarsh almost find 'The Lost Chord' for themselves.

'He was right,' Miss Tidmarsh whispers.

'Who?'

'That drunk. Your life does go too fast. And it doesn't mean anything.'

'Gwen – please listen. I have had an absurd idea. No, please don't interrupt, my dear. I have been wanting to find a moment since we set out on our peregrinations this morning.'

But the celebrated Herr Vincent Bach has stepped squarely forward from the back of the bandstand once more, and the audience is applauding him without enthusiasm, for a second time.

Hurry, Mr Shephard!

'I do not, of course, Gwen, mean to suggest anything at all wrong. I must make that absolutely clear from the start. You know I would never suggest anything wrong. Certainly not to you, for whom, I think you know, I have the utmost respect. But do you think that we – that is, you and I – could – ?'

But the celebrated Herr Bach has begun again. And his cornet and the seagulls are now the saddest sound imaginable this last Edwardian Friday afternoon.

'Ah yes,' Mr Shephard murmurs. 'Sir Arthur's masterpiece.'

And they stay absolutely still, sprawled out on the floor, until the applause.

* * * * *

Just as a common wasp (*Vespula vulgaris*) steers down a breeze from Columbus Ravine, and floats above Percy's bare bum. It purrs gently above the white nates bouncing like two little junkets in unison below. As the July air eddies, so it circles yellow and black, admiring.

As a common English wasp, of course, it has little excuse for being in the newly made Japanese Peasholm Forest. But there is nothing very Japanese here, except that you can see the top of the Japanese Waterfall down in the boating lake, if you lie on your back, like Lizzie is doing.

There is not much privacy, either.

But there is enough.

It is a male wasp now hovering fascinated by the endless strangeness of the natural world. For how complex and patterned this mating seems to be, compared to his own, where the females simply live on through the winter, after they've been done, quickly and fully clothed, leaving their males to die long before Christmas.

Twice he glides low enough to brush Percy's white bum with his wings. Once he lands for the tiniest moment.

Percy and Lizzie know nothing about wasps. (For insurance purposes this might count as personal carelessness. Or encouragement?) They don't even notice this one, during their shared half-hour under the baby trees. They do not even know he is a male wasp, doomed to die as soon as winter. Or, more importantly perhaps, that the male wasp cannot sting you anyway, even if he wants to.

So Percy's much admired bum is safe. And Percy and

Lizzie cannot get distressed by any sudden epiphany or metaphor of their own coming fates, drawn from the private lives and griefs of the common wasp.

So all Lizzie can say after it is, 'I'll never tell her. Till you want me to.'

And when Percy can't find his stud Lizzie swaps his stiff collar for her pink headscarf, and ties it round his sore neck.

'All right, Lizzie?'

'Course. Bit draughty, mind you.'

'Me mam's tablecloth might have helped.'

'Wouldn't have fancied me Christmas pudding round your house, mind you!' And she pulls at her skirt as the wasp flies off.

14

High Tide

Danger! – The burial – Mr Holles tells a story about the death
of the dog last Monday afternoon – The girl in the motor car –
Who's afraid of the high tide? – The lost poem – The ring,
the fish and the wedding – And next?

Ten past four all along both bays. The sea is irritable. The last swimmers climb out of the sea that smacks the Marine Drive and the harbour walls and the Spa and all the crumbling coast from Flamborough to Whitby.

The afternoon's birth will be a hard one. And the crowds are already gathering to watch it all along the sea front.

And the danger flags are up.

* * * * *

Tommy, Spud and Monkey dodge barefoot on what is left of the South Sands.

Tommy spots some sand. 'This'll do.' And they squirm into the spare patch below two Scotch women mending nets on the harbour wall. They line up their boots. 'Hold the flags, Monkey.'

'Yeah, Tommy. What game is it?'

Tommy and Spud dig out an oblong, a foot deep.

'Lie down.'

'Yeah, Tommy.' Monkey curls his legs in but his knees still stick up.

Spud yells, 'Humpty Dumpty sat on a wall, Humpty Dumpty had a great fall.' And he spanks Monkey's knees with the spade.

'Hands together, eyes closed,' Tommy says. 'Not you, Monkey. You want your hands down there.'

'Like he used to have them when he were alive,' Spud says, 'so when folk dig up his skelington they'll find him with his bony fingers clutching his bony thing, and they'll know it's him.'

Tommy says, 'There isn't no bone in your thing.'

There is a delay in the funeral, and you can hear distant hymns among the waves.

Monkey says, 'What do I do, Tommy?'

'Die!' Spud hisses. 'I told you I'd kill you if you come with us, mental.'

'Dust to dust, ashes to ashes, amen. Off you go, grave digger!'

Spud drops wet sand on Monkey's face. 'We should have shut his mouth, if he's dead, like they did with my dad.'

'Stop him, Tommy.'

'There ain't much sand left.'

But there is just enough sand for them to bury Monkey with.

So they do.

* * * * *

And far above South Sands Mr Holles is drinking brandy and inspecting Spaldy the painter up by the Castle.

'Been painting all your beano, Spaldy?'

'Yes, Mr Holles sir.'

'Poor Mrs Holles here has been bilious all hers. Hold this newspaper I've been keeping my memory in order with, using my mnemotechnical studies.' He passes him the afternoon's local paper. 'You try me on this sad story about a dog, Spaldy, then I'll have a look at your painting.'

'Yes, Mr Holles sir.'

Mr Holles recites mnemotechnically, ' "A dog's plight. A fine retriever dog met its death in a curious way on Monday afternoon at Scarborough. It belonged to a waiter at King's Cliff Holiday Camp. The dog tried to get through the gate and was caught on a spike. It was released but the animal died." Word for word, eh?'

'Yes, Mr Holles sir.'

'Very sad that. You'd expect a woman to cry, but poor Mrs Holles has no feelings left. The latest in the Roses matches, by the way, Rhodes ninety-five not out and Yorkshire 312 for six in reply to Lancashire's 249, but you don't need to check that.

We want to have a look at your painting next.'

'Yes, Mr Holles sir.'

Mr Holles waves his two women forward to examine Spaldy's beano landscape. Poor Mrs Holles looks taut and old.

Mr Holles shakes his head at the painting and rubs his finger on the wet paint. 'It's far too bleak.'

'Yes, Mr Holles sir.'

'You want to get yourself a Kodak. Get the sun behind you, click, and you can spend the rest of your day enjoying yourself.'

'Thank you, sir.'

'And I don't see any pier on your picture.'

'Pier, Mr Holles sir?'

'The first Mrs Holles, who now seems to be going mad without me having to go to the expense of putting her in a home first, has a very clear memory of her Liberal father carrying her on a wooden pier. It is from the long ago days when she was happy. She keeps telling the employees about it, surprised she's not told you. The trouble is there isn't any pier like that, judging from your picture and from what we can see.'

'Sir.'

'I notice you've no people on your picture, either.'

'No, sir.'

'Scared of painting human skin, eh? That's what's hardest in painting you see, Girl.'

The Girl curtsies, 'Sir.'

Spaldy says, 'My eyes aren't what they were, Mr Holles.'

'That's with all the stuff we put in the paint at the brewery to make it go further. Still, pays your rent, doesn't it? Here.' He offers his silver flask.

'I don't drink, Mr Holles sir.'

'You do.'

Spaldy nods and drinks.

'Go on, you sup it and enjoy yourself for once, Spaldy. You see human skin and horses are the hardest thing. Tell you what. I'll lend the Girl to you Spaldy when we get back, and you can paint her as Lady Godiva traipsing round Coventry. Two fillies for the price of one. Drink it, Spaldy. I did tell you.'

'Yes sir, thank you sir.' He drinks. And hands it back.

'Never mind, you'll be back doing some real painting tomorrow, eh? And I can't spend all day flattering my workers to stop them joining so-called trades unions. Must get on now. This is reckoned to be a bracing walk. I don't know who's getting braced for what yet, mind you. Come on, Mrs Bilious, or I'll force feed you Zam Buk. Zam Buk is in this paper, Spaldy. It cures pimples, summer skin blotches, scabby sores and ringworm.' He puts out his elbows. 'And you, Miss Godiva.'

* * * * *

And a big open motor car chugs past Lizzie and Percy as they walk through Peasholm Gap towards the sea.

The cocky driver wears goggles, and a blazer. The girl at his side has not even got a hat, and her blonde hair blows free in the breeze that is coming in with the tide.

Lizzie and Percy recognize her.

Lizzie looks away at once, and points at the poster for the Fol-de-Rols at the New Floral Hall where everything is glass and geraniums.

Percy stumbles into Lizzie's hat box. 'Look!'

* * * * *

Mr Shephard and Miss Tidmarsh are looking out at the sea, sitting side by side in their hired yellow-and-black jockey carriage with a passenger brake, on the New Marine Drive. Their gloved hands rest separately on the rug covering their knees. Only five yards of pavement and a fragile iron fence separate them from the splendid high tide now coming in from Europe.

Mr Shephard shouts from the wet guidebook, ' "The Marine Drive was begun in 1897 for the Diamond Jubilee, but in fact – " Why are you crying, Gwenny?'

'Hold me.'

'The workpeople will – '

'Chuff the workpeople.'

The sea leaps as high as a gas lamp.

'Gwen, dear, dear Gwen. Don't you think I would have arranged our affairs differently if they could have been so arranged?'

She hides in his coat. He puts his arm round her.

'They can be, Trevor. I am so frightened. Look at the waves.'

But a few splendid waves do not frighten the Chapel folk still singing hymns in South Bay.

Besides, God knows what He is doing.

For today the splendid waves have pushed the hymn-singing further and further up the sands until it is now on the Foreshore Road itself, spilling out as far as the trams, and delaying them. The trippers, who have been forced off the beach with nothing to do but to stand scoffing at the singing, have quickly recognized a tune they know, and have stayed to join in.

The earth is being filled with the Glory of God, as the waters cover the sea.

> 'I am resting so sweetly in Jesus now
> I sail the wide sea no more
> The tempest may sweep o'er the wild storm so deep
> I am safe when the storm comes no more
> I have enclosed my soul in the haven of rest,
> I sail the wide seas no more,
> The tempest may sweep o'er the wild stormy deep
> But in Jesus I'm safe ever more.'

* * * * *

But the tempest does sweep this afternoon.

The waters thrash and just fail to climax. Then one wave in twenty, thirty even, pushes in from far out, gathers the energy of all the others before it and lashes and smashes itself into an ecstasy that spurts up, twice as high as the gas lamps.

Nothing more exciting happens all holiday!

Alone you would be terrified, for this high tide comes from your nightmares when sudden waves leap and suffocate you without giving you time to hold your breath.

But together, here, we can huddle and shriek and pretend we are only pretending to be frightened.

* * * * *

Seven minutes to high tide. There is a false quiet. And then the most terrible wave of the afternoon rips the air and smashes across Marine Drive. It knocks a horse on to the railings and the horse bolts towards Scalby Mills.

* * * * *

Albert and Flossie are caught by the sea on the wrong side of

South Bay. They cannot get through the hymn singers and the trams, so they stand by the sandy, bandstandy entrance to the People's Palace, leaning on the bars and hoping to see some late drownings.

'You know that poem of mine, Floss?' Albert yells.

'Aye.'

'I've forgot all the words again.'

'It'll be the ale, they don't know how to keep it, see.'

* * * * *

And even now this high tide that washes away poems and horses is not over.

Look, Lizzie is standing among the more nervous crowds on the land side of the road and North Bay. She watches Percy being suicidal in her headscarf.

'I'm standing here till you tell me if it were Bunty in that motor car.'

'Course it were then.'

'And Mr Holles's nephew in them glasses?'

'Course.'

Percy turns to the North Sea, and screams at it.

A wave three times his height leaps over him.

But, when Lizzie dares to look, Percy is walking back towards her, with his hair down his forehead, like it must be first thing of a morning.

She grabs his wrist. 'Thought we'd lost you then, love.'

'How could she do it, Lizzie?'

'She's going to marry him. He asked her Whit Sunday at the Sings.'

'When I went fishing at Worksop.'

'She's been seeing him Monday nights.'

'She were reckoned to be round her grandma's.'

Another wave drops on them, but they do not notice.

'She give herself till the beano to choose, Percy. And she's chose.'

'And gone round in motor cars with him all day while I've wasted my beano fretting for her.'

'I kept telling you.'

'I got her a chuffing engagement ring, it's in me pocket somewhere here. I'll chuck it in them waves and them chuffing fish can eat it. And when she's wed to Mester chuffing Atkinson I hope she chokes on it eating chuffing fish with him at her wedding.'

But he shakes his head, and does not chuck the ring anywhere.

'I could have been fishing today.'

'Aye, love.'

One last wave soaks them.

'When her mother finds out tomorrow what's been going on – '

'She knows. And Bunty's staying all week.'

'It's not fair.'

'No.' Lizzie picks up her hat box. 'Anyroad, thanks for doing me, Percy.'

'Where you going?'

'If you don't have to tell folk about you and me in the bushes, Percy, don't, there's a love?'

'Where are you going?'

'You don't want me.'

* * * * *

Nineteen minutes past five.

And it is suddenly not high tide any more.

Weekly guests who have felt the pull of oceans apologize for all the excitement and ask each other what time they will need to be off in the morning.

Day-trippers shake themselves dry and set off for the trains.

The North Sea swirls under the Marine Drive, ashamed of its showing off, and skulks back to Europe, to make a fuss there.

* * * * *

Less than an hour and a half to the fuzzy photograph now.

The photographer is the small man already struggling up Valley Road to the excursion station, with his tripod, frames, camera, plates, and cloth. He does not seem to be nervous yet. Though he will be.

Odd, isn't it though? As far as we know nobody has been drowned yet, but plenty of us won't be on the nervous photograph where Mrs Holles is smiling behind the terrified rows of railway workers in uniform.

So the beano's not quite over, even now?

PART SIX

15

The Last Hour

The suffragettes use their vote – The view from the Grand –
What the painter cannot see, however hard he looks – Poverty
and poetry and beer and sunshine and a silver fourpenny bit –
Dancing in the dark – The long climb home.

Five-and-twenty to six, and the crowds are climbing up from the sea.

And two suffragettes from Washing slap each other dry in that funny wooden shelter at the bottom of St Nicholas' Gardens.

'That were a real nice walk on that beach, Ada, a real nice paddle and a real nice wet.'

'You've been a bit low today, Bess, till now like?'

'Best day of the year and all, eh?'

'Your old man still?'

'Kind of.'

'He didn't treat you right, Bess.'

'Course he didn't.'

'Though I'll never know what he saw in Edna.'

'Oh I do, but what we talking about men for anyroad? We're suffragettes, aren't we?'

And they hug.

'Fancy a port and lemon, to warm us up?'

'Aye. And some winkles for the journey. If suffragettes is allowed winkles.'

'That reminds me. We'd best find Edna. She'll still be in that arcade with them mucky pictures.'

And she is, though she has not enjoyed them since poor Mrs Holles told her all about Mr Holles down at the harbour.

And anyway, she's long since spent up.

When Ada and Bess arrive, laughing and still wet, she

grumbles at being kept here so long waiting. But she does not tell them about poor Mrs Holles. She asks Ada for some coppers from the kitty.

'For a present.'

'Who for?'

'The old man. Just summat little.'

'Your old man's got something little already, didn't you say, Bess?' Ada winks.

'From what I remember.'

Edna stares at them. Bess and – her old man?

Bess says, 'We're suffragettes, what's it matter? We're spending up on port and lemon and winkles and eye-tiddly-eye-tie ice cream and two ounces of Tom Thumb mixture in a cone each – down the Underground Palace.'

'We're not suffragettes,' Edna shouts. 'We know nowt about suffragettes. Never met none, never read owt about none either. We're just three daft women who reckon to have come to have a good time. And I want to get my husband a souvenir.'

Ada nods. 'Aye well, since we are suffragettes it's votes for women we believe in so we'll use us votes. Spend up on us-se'ns, vote now.' She and Bess raise their hands. 'Spending on her little husband with the little winkle?' Edna does not even bother to vote.

'I'm not sitting with you two miseries on the way home, missing all the fun,' Edna says.

'We'll vote on that, too, when the time comes,' Ada says. 'Come on, let's get on that front and spend.'

* * * * *

Bunty in her double bedroom at the Grand Hotel can see the suffragettes running arm-in-arm along the front towards the Underground People's Palace. She stands, alone and barefoot, looking out from her great window, rubbing her yellow hair with a long soft towel. Her fingers are wrinkled from the deepest bath of her life.

She hears no sound through the heavy glass. It is as if she is now watching Scarborough itself on the pictures. And she has already been to the pictures twice today. (She liked *The Sacrifice of Kathleen* at the Palladium Picture House best, because it was sad.)

It's Lizzie she's looking for really. Though she does not expect to see her, even though Lizzie did promise last night, when they agreed to swap Percy, that she would let her know what had happened. But she does not expect to be seeing much of Percy or Lizzie from now on anyway. Hers will be a new life with Mr Atkinson . . . Bound to take some getting used to . . .

She drops her towel and stares at herself without blinking in the great golden mirror. She is too beautiful for Percy and the Hop Stores, isn't she? And Mr Atkinson – Alan – and his family and friends eat different and drink different and sleep different . . . They live longer, and they don't get old so soon.

Bunty sips her green drink. It tastes of peppermint and burnt apples. She does not like it.

But it's all going to take some getting used to.

She stares on at herself, still not blinking.

* * * * *

Spaldy the painter is staring through the ha'penny telescope, swinging it too fast to see anything properly, as if there is no time any more.

He does not see the three suffragettes from Washing paying to go down into the People's Palace where mermaids sing in halls of laughter, and the Electric Lady is amazing, and the free dance floor is serviced with an efficient orchestra.

* * * * *

He does not see Mr Holles explode champagne all over poor Mrs Holles and the Grand Hotel terrace. And console his nephew Alan by telling him of his own honeymoon. And explode another bottle for Alan, just downstairs after an hour galloping his blonde filly, and looking as if he's earned it.

Spaldy does not see poor Mrs Holles go upstairs to change. But before she does, she goes to the Girl's double bedroom instead, to tell her to run away, now, before it is too late, and to give her some money. But the door is unlocked, and all that is left of the Girl is her uniform neatly folded on the bed.

Spaldy does not see poor Mrs Holles come out of the bedroom and bump into the young wine waiter from lunch, waiting in the corridor. He apologizes and offers her a real photograph picture postcard of the wooden pleasure pier in North Bay! With its refreshment saloon at the end, stretching a thousand yards out into the North Sea, far beyond the waves! Just like a bridge! Until the freak wave of 1905 that washed it away.

Spaldy does not see Mrs Holles hold the young wine waiter's hand. And laugh.

* * * * *

Spaldy does not see the Girl, in her own clothes, looking at her gold watch as she chugs along the coast in the coast train to Whitby.

Or Monkey, buried with full military honours down by the harbour.

Or Percy and Lizzie, sharing their first pot of tea in the café at the corner by Peasholm Gap.

Or Owen.

Or Flossie finding one trouser-leg while looking with Albert for the nearest Britlings pub to the harbour.

* * * * *

Spaldy pushes the telescope away before his ha'penny runs out. Mr Holles's brandy has made him jumpy. He squeezes ointment from the tube into the corner of his eye and blinks. He picks up his wet painting and begins the long climb down to the harbour, and the real painters.

* * * * *

The real painters now in fact are outside a Britlings pub, a fish-head's throw from the harbour.

'One for the worms?'

'I'll force one, Albie.'

Albert blows his nose with his fingers and bumps through the early evening drinkers into the brown stench of the dock-side pub. A pickpocket feels the thick wad of *The Times* newspaper in his back pocket, mistakes it for more money than Albert has ever had in all his life, and steals it. Albert does not care. He will not need it now.

The sun outside is very bright. Flossie put his hands over his eyes and thinks of the crow's-nest boy on the *Titanic*. His cap drops off behind him.

He grabs for it without turning, sways, belches and notices a ragged child without boots, dripping sand and holding out his palm.

'What do you want, lad?' he gasps.

'I've just done me poem, mester.'

'Love poems, me.'

' "Pretty children at your door who never wore nothing",' Monkey bluffs, ' "We need holidays amen see and pity the children" and I've lost my dad and my boots and my pals, mester.'

Flossie clutches Monkey to his damp beer-belly. 'Don't be ashamed, lad.'

'They buried me, mester, and me boots.'

'I'm not ashamed. I'm still standing up, more or less. And me and little Albie are still pals. You think on that word pals, lad.'

'Yes, mester. Mester?' Monkey holds up his palm.

'Men can love each other. I want to die with my pal, I do.'

'Yes, mester.'

Monkey picks up the lost cap and gets another harder hug.

'That's him, there, coming out spilling us beer.' And Flossie goes to Albert and takes the beer to spill it for himself, and explains Monkey. 'It's a poem about pretty children, Albie my old pal. Now we was pretty children once, wasn't we? Off you go, lad.'

Monkey recites with his nose pressed into the 'assels of Flossie's damp white scarf.

'Good stuff, eh?'

'It's Britlings, Floss, what do you expect?'

'This lad's poems, chuff-head.' And he adds, 'We might be working men, lad, but we know poetry and poverty. All right, they might sound the same, poetry and poverty. But they're different, lad. You think on that while Albert sinks his pint and then does some reciting in return for yours.'

'No thanks, mester.' Monkey breaks free.

And Albert shakes his head, distressed. 'I can't, Floss. I can't remember me words no more. There's summat else filling up me head.'

'Ah well,' Flossie says. He tosses a coin at Monkey. 'Take that, remembrance of us, lad.'

'It's a silver one, mester!'

'Britlings' beano 1914. Poverty and poetry! And beer and sunshine! And a silver fourpence to spend on spice for your journey home.'

'Ta, mester. I've not been given no silver one all day.' And he dashes barefoot through the dockside crowds, before Flossie can change his mind.

Flossie peers up from under his cap at the great white sun. 'All over now then, bar the ride, Albie. Flobbed up and nowt to show for it. Wish it were still last Friday? When we'd still got it all to look forward to?' He puts his arm over his little pal's shoulder. Beer splashes over them both.

They drink in warm unison.

Two pints later Flossie says, 'One trouser-leg, eh? I reckon there's something right sad about one trouser-leg.'

But Albert only stares at the sun.

* * * * *

Only thirty-five minutes of beano left now. Poverty and poetry and beer and sunshine and a silver fourpence – and dancing!

Underground dancing, too, in the damp brick Aquarium where the efficient orchestra services the free dance floor.

Edna is dancing. With Bess.

'Don't hold me hand so tight it hurts my fingers, Edna.'

'Well, I'm the man so I do the leading.'

'Not when you're dancing with a suffragette you don't.'

* * * * *

And look among the other couples waltzing free under the streets. Isn't that couple slowly circumnavigating the floor from Britlings? Miss Tidmarsh and Mr Shephard! Holding each other at last in the safest place in Yorkshire. ('Not quite us' indeed!)

'I must say I'm rather surprised you dance, Trevor.'

'Yes, so am I really. Though I did have lessons as a young man.'

'Did you?'

'She was a Miss Glatt with letters. She instructed me in the drawing-room at home while Mummy watched and a second Miss Glatt, who was a niece I believe, played our piano rather heavily.' He treads on her. 'I'm terribly sorry. I'm afraid despite the best endeavours of the Misses Glatt I still cannot waltz and talk at one and the same time.'

They begin again. And they steer right round. Without accident, though Miss Tidmarsh does most of the cornering. She says, 'Could *I* talk, Trevor?' He nods. 'First of all then I wish to apologize for my behaviour today. I have been so very neurasthenic – '

'No, no Gwen, please. You are the very – sorry.'

They begin again.

Half a circuit later he says, 'I've had the wiffle-waffles myself, Gwen, because I've been wanting to say something to you all day. Sorry.'

They begin again.

She says, 'One looks forward to it for so long and then it's suddenly happening and one finds out one's still not ready.' She is aware of her ripped stocking, her squashed hat, her wet clothes, her bruised arm and the tightness of her dead mother's ring. And the two photographs where there should only have been one.

And they have stopped dancing again, though the efficient orchestra's still playing their waltz far away under the wet brick arches.

'Gwen,' he says. 'Please let me finish. I have been trying to ask you something all day. Please let me say what it is, whatever happens.'

Nothing does.

So he speaks. 'Shall we stay tonight?'

He's asked her! At last! And not quite the question we'd thought! Good old Mercury. The sea ceaseth. Unlock every piano in Yorkshire. The world is new. Start the Russian Revolution three years early. Listen for the sound of the great Amen.

Choose what metaphor you want.

But Mr Shephard is already adding, 'We could return tomorrow by the morning service train. We would not be recognized, for most of the workpeople will be back at their work, and certainly not out in the streets in the morning. I've brought enough extra money. We could find a hotel on the North Side and – no. It's a very selfish idea. And a very wrong one. Please forget I asked, Miss Tidmarsh.'

* * * * *

Spaldy stumbles alone back up King's Cliff, smudging his wet oil painting. At the top he rubs his eyes for one last look at the sea that is halfway down the beach again. Just like it was when we first saw it. Might as well not have come.

There is an autumn smell of dying roses and newly dug earth.

* * * * *

And only twenty minutes to the train now.

Bunty, wrapped in her soft Grand Hotel towel, stares down at the Front.

But she does not see Percy walking hand-in-hand with Lizzie, with Percy wearing the scarf and carrying the hat box.

For Bunty is crying.

And she isn't even going home.

159

16

The Ghost Train

Mr Wagstaff versus the stowaways – The suffragettes find a haven – Poor Mrs Holles – A song about a sailor, sung while eating crabs – The great share-out – The pipe-smokers go home – Miss Tidmarsh and Mr Shephard begin recuperating – The speech and the photographs and the fireworks – Missing – All aboard for the ghost train.

'Third Class employees are required to proceed along the platform but to refrain from boarding the train until the departure ceremonials have been completed. The train is rostered to leave in fifteen minutes.' Mr Wagstaff is very brisk in his mackintosh on a table halfway up Platform 2 at the excursion station.

But stand as close as this to him and you can smell whisky when he sneezes and points his megaphone at you. A length of black indiarubber tube dangles from his coat pocket. 'Britlings Breweries hope you have had a recreational and educational day and have a safe and sensible journey home. That journey will begin in fifteen minutes.' He turns and points the megaphone towards the entrance. 'You are further reminded of the bun and beer issue at York –'

But he's seen the stowaways, Tommy, Spud – and Monkey, just back from the dead with fourpence-worth of spice for the journey.

'You're that Tommy, lad.'

'Me, Mester Wagstaff?'

'Aaaaagh!' And Monkey has his fit.

It doesn't work.

Mr Wagstaff calls, 'Your father does not work at Britlings, Tommy.'

Spud from behind Monkey calls, 'Least he's got a father, Waggy.'

Tommy clutches at his trousers. 'Give over Spud, we've all got to get home yet.' And he adds, 'I'm not me, mester.'

Mr Wagstaff calls, 'And his father is not a Britlings employee neither.'

A drunken clogger, with no teeth but still tasting blood, walks over Monkey's bare feet. Monkey cannot shout because he is still having his fit for Tommy.

* * * * *

And Bess and Ada arm-in-arm Edna up the platform, looking for their Ladies Only. They're all tingly with port and lemon and the wind and the sea. And, though they spend their lives washing, they do not notice that the scarlet-and-green train has been washed and polished as new as this morning, while they've been on their holiday.

'I'll miss all the fun!' Edna shouts.

'We've had plenty of fun today without needing men for it.'

'It's not been like a beano at all.'

'No, we didn't get drunk and we didn't get pregnant for once. But me and Bess had a grand walk all along that sea. Vote we push her in here, Bess?'

'Me too.'

But when they look inside the Ladies Only they find there is a new lady there – and a toothy baby – breast feeding. 'Never stop, do they, bless them?'

Ada asks if the baby's a boy or a lady.

And she's a lady. So they all sit down and take their shoes off.

And when the men poke in in a while to order everyone to get off and have their photo taken, all five ladies will stay where they are. They are not being ordered by men any more, are they, not on the beano anyway. They share the winkles.

(And that's why they are not on this beano photograph, of course.)

* * * * *

161

But what about the stowaways?

Spud is yelling at Waggy. 'You got Tommy barred from going to Blackpool with your lot, Waggy, and he'd wasted millions of Sundays at your church!'

Mr Wagstaff sneezes. 'That heathen broke our window.'

'Tell you, I'm not me.'

Passing excursionists grin. Waggy gets his mad up every beano, when he's been drinking. It's with him being teetotal.

'I'm having a fit again, Mr Waggy!' Monkey smacks his head on the platform.

Spud shouts, 'He only bust your window after, Waggy, you chuffing chuff!'

And just listen now to Mr Wagstaff screaming like a woman from Washing. 'You are not coming back in my train. You are not insured. And those of us with adequate vocabularies would prefer – '

But look who's interrupting him now!

'More wrinkles on your arse, Waggy?'

'Sir.'

Mr Holles has arrived by dog cart from the Grand. With poor Mrs Holles. He shouts, 'Had an enjoyable day here, you lads?'

'Sir.' Spud and Tommy mumble, waiting to be hit.

But Monkey looks up at poor Mrs Holles. 'Mester Waggy won't let us go home, mester. And I never seen the sea only I have now and I've got to go home, mester, or me mam'll crack me. And I've lost me boots.'

Mr Holles peers, trying to focus, uneasy that he can't remember where all this has happened before. He grabs the megaphone, and pokes the fat end at Mr Wagstaff. 'You look peaky after your holiday, Waggy, you old fart-catcher. And these future employees are quite right. You are a chuff. Run along lads and get yourselves some nice seats.' He waves. 'And what of poor Mrs Holles's nice seat, eh, my seagull?' And he strokes her bum.

And Mrs Holles says loudly, 'You are drunk, Mr Holles.'

Mr Holles jerks round. Who is this woman, talking to him like that? And going on talking even when he glares at her?

'I have not been bilious since first thing this morning, Mr Holles, and that was because – '

'Because what?'

But she shakes her head. She's not going to tell him. She's never going to tell him.

And she is smiling.

'Well it's no use you standing there like you've just seen your own arsehole, madam. Go and eat some – some –' He struggles, staring red-eyed over the megaphone. And just remembers. 'That ointment in the paper that's good for, er, spots and, er –'

'Zam Buk,' Mrs Holles says.

'Yes – Zam Buk – yes.' He stares at her, aware that something is terribly wrong. She is smiling at him. He rocks, and turns back to Mr Wagstaff. 'This speech for me table?'

'Sir.'

'My Girl turned up yet with her gold watch – what's it called?'

'No, Mr Holles sir.'

'What about that lord mayoress who liked me?'

'No, sir.'

'Drabble-tailed whores.' He shakes his head, confused. 'Is that dwarf with the towel the photographer?'

'Sir.'

'Get him photographing then. I've had enough.'

'Sir.'

Mr Wagstaff looks at Mrs Holles. He winks for the third time. He is looking strangely cheerful.

He seems to say, 'We are the meek and the dying. We betray ourselves and each other so that he will be kind to us, though he never will be again.' But Mr Wagstaff looks very cheerful about it. It's the end of the beano. He is going home. 'But,' he seems to say to Mrs Holles, 'your children and grandchildren will be Holles's for ever.'

Mrs Holles shakes her head at that.

Just as her fading husband shouts, 'This megaphone smells of brandy, Waggy. That you or me?' And he biffs him with it.

'It's for my cold I seem to have caught, sir,' Mr Wagstaff says. 'And it's whisky, sir.'

* * * * *

The jolly electricians and their jolly wives begin to sing 'Bollocky Bill the Sailor' as they crunch crabs on a railway bench.

* * * * *

In an empty Third Class that smells of babies Tommy does the dip for the spice.

> 'Ip dip dip my blue ship
> Sailing on the water
> Like a cup and saucer
> You are going to be it.'

Monkey says, 'I like the sea now when I've seen it.'

'You're mental, you.'

'I know, Tommy.'

'We'll bury you proper next year.'

'Yeah, Tommy. And I can be a ghost.'

'There aren't any ghosts bar the Holy Ghost. And he's not a ghost.'

'Mental,' Spud says.

'Who is?'

'All on us.'

* * * * *

Spaldy and the ancient blacksmith sit alone in the Third Class carriage three doors down. Their carriage smells of oil paint and tobacco. Nobody wants to smell that all the way home, so they will sit alone all the way back, biting their pipes and hardly talking. And when they do they will not talk about Spaldy's eyes. Or the blacksmith's lost strength. Or their coming poverty.

'First smoke I've had all day.'

'Aye. You want to tamp it down more.'

'I had to reckon up if it were worth spending on a new pipe. I'm not young.'

'Bugger, isn't it?'

'Is that, lad.'

* * * * *

Mr Wagstaff passes the window, megaphoning. They ignore him, though most employees who have already got on the train, with their bottles and fish and songs and souvenirs, get out again for the photograph once he has passed.

Late sunshine dapples through the fretted excursion roof where the seagulls sit. Still laughing. And trying to decide whether to be on the photograph or not.

* * * * *

164

Not everyone will be on the photograph, of course. For there are only three more minutes of beano left now.

Miss Tidmarsh and Mr Shephard are not here. Though nobody notices.

Owen isn't here, in red tie and sandals.

And a contralto and tenor are missing from the Chapel party in the very back carriage.

* * * * *

But look now at Mr Holles, poking Mr Wagstaff's trousers with his paper.

'Yorkshire 312 for 6, so all's not lost in England, Waggy.'

'Sir.'

'Those ragged-arsed victims were right about you, mind you. Chuff you were, are and ever more will be so.'

'Sir.'

'Can't even organize a piss-up in the brewery.' And then, 'We'll have my speech, photograph, flowers for madam, and the fireworks, and off you go.'

'Sir.'

'Mrs Holles here could do with a firework up here. You never married, Waggy?'

'No, sir.'

'Not that much of a chuff then. My compliments to your member for Cockshire, wherever he's hiding in these trousers. Now then, Mrs Holles, what are you smiling for? Hoping I'll not start the farewell speech with "Dear Britlings slaves"? But shall I spread a little Liberalism for you? "Dear fellow-workers at Britlings who co-operate each day to get poorer and older making things people wouldn't want in a better society"? That's what your father no doubt said when he brought you to Scarborough as a girl and carried you down the wooden pier that doesn't exist. But he always was a cheating Liberal. Whoeeo!'

Mr Holles sways, and holds his head. Mrs Holles smiles.

Mr Wagstaff calls, 'Are you certain you feel well, enough to make a speech, sir? Mr Holles?'

'I'm drunk, Waggy, thank God. Help me on to the table. And we'll have the first Mrs Holles up here as well, so the sparged workers can look at her arse, while I tell them off about trade unionitis.'

But Mrs Holles is still smiling.

* * * * *

And Miss Tidmarsh and Mr Shephard are clinking glasses of fizzy white ginger beer in the electrically lit Temperance Bar down in the Aquarium. The guidebooks are under their tall stools, being left behind.

'Do you realize, Gwen, that we have not in fact eaten all day since the mint imperials this morning?'

'I am aware of feeling rather light-headed. Almost giddy.'

They drink white ginger beer.

'What are you looking at, Trevor?'

'Your eyes, Gwen. I've never . . . I am so sorry. But if I may say . . . I have never noticed your eyes before.'

Miss Tidmarsh whimpers. What a pickle!

They drink.

'Trevor?'

She takes off her glove to show him her mother's wedding ring. On her own rather red wedding finger.

He does not understand.

She explains. He blushes. She blushes.

But it does not matter now. They've all night to recuperate.

And ginger beer has never tasted naughtier than it does this evening, ten minutes after the train has gone.

* * * * *

Except it hasn't.

For Mr Holles has only just got to the serious part of his speech. Though Mrs Holles is still smiling.

'So-called unionitisitis!' he denounces. And he goes on to outline the ruination by politics of family businesses like his by men like Mr Lloyd George, though he cannot remember his name.

'And as for those Liberals like him,' Mr Holles struggles, 'I realize I need the men as much as you need me. And the women, bless you. And the little children, and all our children living happily for ever and ever amen, full of Britlings Bitter from morning till night.'

But Mrs Holles still smiles.

'And to conclude,' he concludes, 'I do not of course wish on this festive occasion to be controverted. Contrabanded. Controversial. Britlings is best! So say "beer", and don't move.Don't even bl— bl— bl— move your eyes up or down.'

They do and don't (blink).

But Mr Holles now insists that the driver, fireman, guard and all the Scarborough excursion staff who are correctly enough dressed join the photograph. The clenched excursionists wait without moving. Mr Holles abuses the railway staff for the strokes, which he then corrects to strikes, of last year, and he arranges them in the front row very near the camera.

'Now!'

And the magnesium explodes. And at last the railway men are blinded.

* * * * *

And this is how the beano always ends, with the photograph on the station. You cannot be sure who's not here, because the cameraman is nervous. But wouldn't you be, with Mr Holles drunk and angry a few yards in front of you? And no wonder the railway workers in their smart uniforms in the front row look so terrified as they wait to be blinded.

The porky party from Electric Light and their porky wives do look too jolly. And the Chapel folk do look too sober, after their long day of teetotal singing. Though even they aren't all present are they, when you count them?

Who else isn't here?

The suffragettes? They're picnicking in the Ladies Only.

The Carpentry Shop? They never got beyond York this morning.

And Owen, the Clarion socialist, who had to choose between revolution and oatcakes, and doesn't seem to be coming home at all? (Those two lopsided drunks, of course, are Albert and Flossie, his mates from the Paint Shop, next to Percy from Cooperage who is holding hands with that Lizzie from Hop Stores, who has lent him her pink headscarf because of his collar.)

And that huge man pointing his finger into his wide-open mouth must be the purple clogger who still had three teeth left this morning.

And that is probably the widow from the pub next to the cemetery, with her hand on the arm of Mr Wagstaff in his mackintosh, with his board saying 'Britlings 1914', and looking far too cheerful for him. But why shouldn't he be cheerful? It's all over. And half a bottle of whisky is still sinning away inside him.

But Mr Holles does look desperate on his table in the very middle of the fuzzy photograph, as if he has glimpsed some sudden unthinkable future.

Has Mrs Holles just smilingly whispered to him to go and eat some Zam Buk? Or is it just because she is smiling? About her postcard of Scarborough's lost wooden pier? Now tucked into her bag, no doubt, as she plans the rest of her life . . .

Thirteen minutes to seven, and odd!

* * * * *

Anyway, odd or not the railway men are blinded. Then there is a thick black cloud, and smuts fall everywhere. There are screams and a pause, and then a great scramble back to the train. Nobody gives orders. And that is the oddest thing of all the beano. It is finally a porter who shouts amid the shambles, 'All aboard for your ghost train.' And a whistle blows.

A great firework explodes at the back of the train. The pigeons shriek in their baskets. The clock shakes. Seagulls scream everywhere. There is a sudden enormous cloud from the green engine, thrown back over its shoulder down the scarlet train and all over the excursion platform. And, a long time after it should have left, the train does.

'You look right white, Albie.'

'Aye, Floss.'

'Like you're seeing ghosts.'

And then, 'Here, it's moving. Wait for us!' Flossie grabs Albert and tugs him to the platform edge as the train sidles past. The very last carriage door is open.

And a Chapel man grabs Albert and pulls him in, and Flossie dives in after.

The Chapel man says, 'We've lost a contralto and a tenor. I hope you two good people can sing.'

* * * * *

Hardly anyone bothers to look out of the windows now for a last view of the station, and Mr Holles, and the Queen of the Watering Places.

The beano is over. Off with your boots. Do what you want, now.

Except in the very back carriage, of course. For Albert and Flossie have been given a spare hymn book each. Flossie cannot read, and his cap keeps falling off so that he doesn't get into trouble. Albert's lips move, though his words are different from those of the singing Chapel folk.

> 'See o'er the foaming billows fair haven's land,
> Drear was the voyage now almost o'er,
> Safe within the lifeboat sailor
> Pull for the shore,
> Heed not the rolling waves
> But bend to the oars.
> Safe within the lifeboat cling to self no more,
> Leave the poor old stranded wreck
> And pull for the shore.'

Flossie whispers, ' "Poor old stranded wreck", Albie. They're singing about us.'

But Albert grips Flossie's arm. 'Listen!' And he recites under the hymn. ' "Down the close darkening lanes they sang their way to the siding shed and lined the train with faces grimly gay." '

Flossie says, 'Give over, Albie love. We've still got the beer and bun to look forward to at York.'

'Listen, Flossie! "Their breasts were stuck all white with wreaths and spray as men's are dead dull porters watch them and the casual tramp stood staring hard sorry to miss them from the upland camp then unmoved signals nodded and a lamp winked at the guard." '

'It's only a poem, Albie!'

' "So secretly like wrongs hushed up they went." Listen!'

'You're tearing my beano suit.'

'It *is* a poem, Floss. But it's not one they learned me at school.'

'Aye, well.'

'I've never been learned it. It's just in my head. What's happening?'

'We're going home, pal,' Flossie says. He holds his pal's hand. But he is suddenly terrified too.

It must be the beer.

* * * * *

All aboard for the ghost train, eh?

In ten days' time not all the king's horses and all the king's men will be able to put things together again.

The sand's run out.

* * * * *

There are a few incidents on the way back.

There is a shambles with the beer and buns at York.

But the carpenters who have spent all day playing farthing brag on York Station now rejoin the singing, cuddling beano, and say what a good time they have had, thanks to the draught Britlings on Platform 3.

The train is one-and-a-half hours late home.

But the band is still waiting, to repeat 'God Save The King', and to be paid.

The beano unpacks itself.

There is a small crowd waiting, including Mrs E. There is a lot of hugging. The stumbling excursionists, some flushed, pat the brewery horses and scatter homewards, saying what a grand time they've had and what a card Mr Holles is. And see you at work tomorrow. And there's always Christmas to look forward to, eh, and where shall we go next year?

No one thanks swaying Mr Wagstaff. He doesn't care. It's over. And he's drunk.

The Station Master cradles his sleeping daughter and points to the stars above the station lamps.

'It's going to be a lovely July day tomorrow.'

* * * * *

But that's not much help to us, is it?